The Invisible Riviera

Paul West

Onager Editions
Ithaca, New York

Onager Editions
PO Box 849
Ithaca, New York 14851-0849

The Invisible Riviera
Paul West

Copyright © 2013 by Paul West
ALL RIGHTS RESERVED

First Printing – August 2013
ISBN: 978-1-60047-862-8
Library of Congress Control Number: 2013937933

This book is a work of fiction. Any references to historical events, real people or real locales, names, characters, descriptions, places, and incidents are either the product if the author's imagination or are used fictitiously. Any resemblance to actual events or locales or persons, living or dead, is unintended and entirely coincidental.

No part of this book may be reproduced in any form, by photocopying or any electronic or mechanical means, including information storage or retrieval systems, without permission in writing from the copyright owner, except in the case of brief quotations embodied in critical articles and reviews.

Cover artwork by Paul West

Printed and bound in the United States of America

First Edition

0 1 2 3 4 5 6 7 8

About Paul West

He now lives in Ithaca, New York. ("I'm a country boy, born and bred," he says, "I like trees and lawns, animals and huge silence.") West has been the recipient of numerous prizes and awards, including the Aga Khan Prize in 1974, a National Endowment for the Arts Fellowship in 1979 and 1985, the Hazlett Award for Excellence in the Arts in 1981, the Literature Award from the American Academy and Institute of Arts and Letters in 1985, a 1993 Lannan Prize for Fiction, and the Grand-Prix Halpèrine-Kaminsky for the Best Foreign Book in 1993. In 1994, the Graduate Schools of the Northeast gave West their Distinguished Teaching Award. He has also been named a Literary Lion by the New York Public Library and a Chevalier of the Order of Arts and Letters by the French Government. *The Tent of Orange Mist* was runner-up for the 1996 National Book Critics Circle Fiction Prize and the Nobel Prize for Literature. He's working on his fifty-first book.

BOOKS BY PAUL WEST

FICTION

The Shadow Factory
The Immensity of the Here and Now
Cheops
A Fifth of November
O.K.
The Dry Danube
Life with Swan
Terrestrials
Sporting with Amaryllis
The Tent of Orange Mist
Love's Mansion
The Women of Whitechapel and Jack the Ripper
Lord Byron's Doctor
The Place in Flowers Where Pollen Rests
The Universe, and Other Fictions
Rat Man of Paris
The Very Rich Hours of Count von Stauffenberg
Gala
Colonel Mint
Caliban's Filibuster
Bela Lugosi's White Christmas
I'm Expecting to Live Quite Soon
Alley Jaggers
Tenement of Clay
Now, Voyager

NONFICTION

The Left Hand is the Dreamer
My Father's War
Tea with Osiris
Oxford Days
Master Class
New Portable People
The Secret Lives of Words
My Mother's Music
A Stroke of Genius
Sheer Fiction-Volumes I, II, III, IV
Portable People
Out of My Depths: A Swimmer in the Universe
Words for a Deaf Daughter
I, Said the Sparrow
The Wine of Absurdity
The Snow Leopard
The Modern Novel
Byron and the Spoiler's Art
James Ensor

The Invisible Riviera

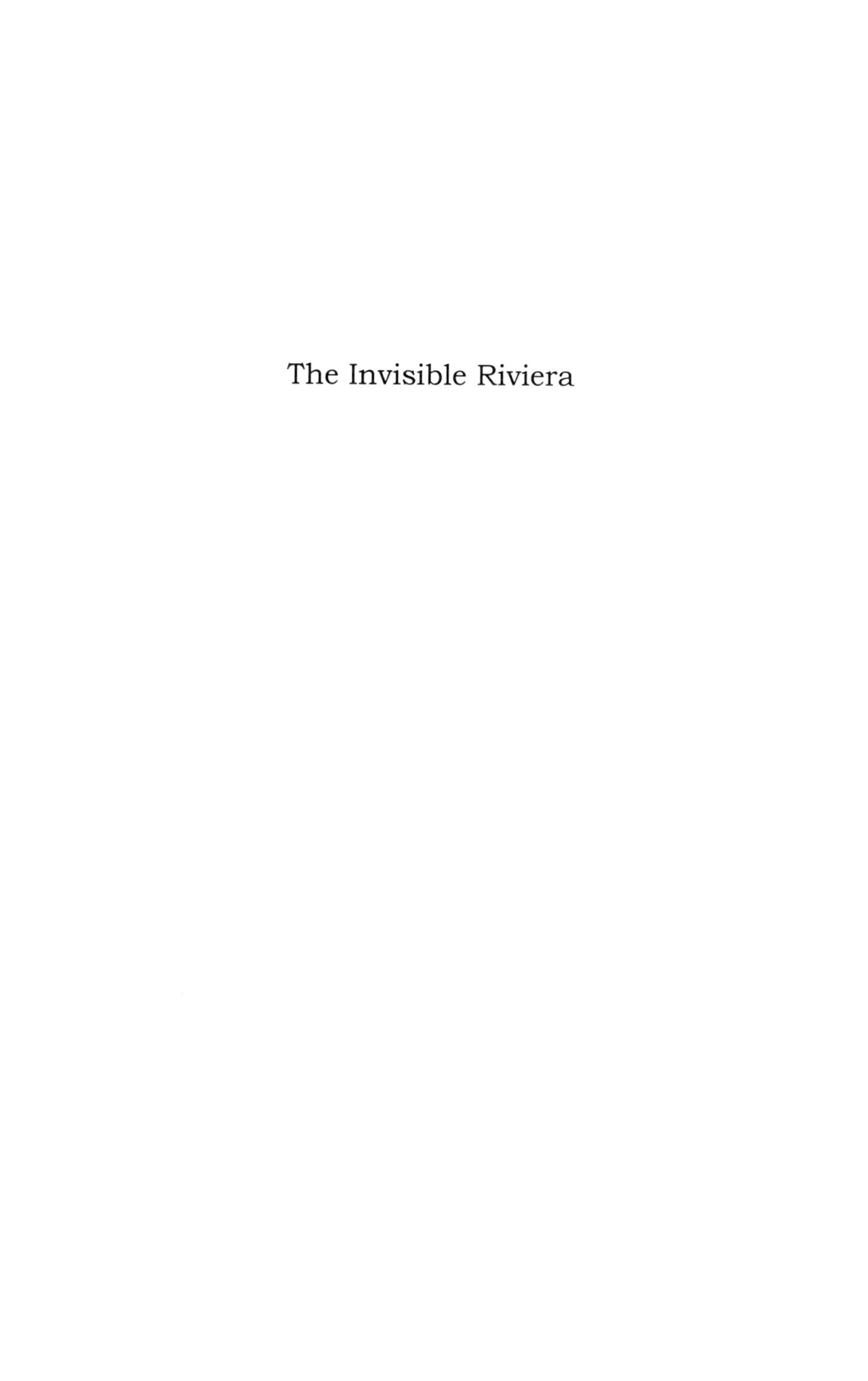

ONE

Enrico Fermi famously asked, "Where is everyone else?" He meant the inhabitants of other galaxies, of course. "Patience," I would have said, had I known him, but I sensed what he meant. That kind of slavering impatience knows no bounds. He was a world traveler, anxious to have it all laid bare in one lifetime, like my friend Light Lomax.

Light wanted the world speeded up, which was why we found ourselves, presently, in Outer Mongolia, where the locals, pausing to see you sampling a book in a shop, halted their motion and talk and remained in suspension until you had finished, which could take minutes or even hours. The Outer Mongolians' reverence for books—from sacred texts to the worst pornography—argued a fetishism born and bred. They'd done this for centuries, mixing gentility and prudence. All signs of civilization were brought to a halt by the appearance of a book, which had something coy and lazy about it, but one got used to such things, especially when they did nobody any harm. Clearly, books were king in this kingdom and appeared likely to remain so.

Be this as it may, last week our farewells had been brief. A pitcher of red spaghetti sauce over one of white, a tureen of white pasta, moldy eggs, rancid salmon, and black German bread had seen us off to our distant destination, complete with snowshoes, rubber galoshes, and skis. We would not be caught napping by any kind of miscreant weather. At easily seven feet, my travel companion, late of Chernobyl (he appeared to have survived without contamination), towered over me as we left, and threw his shadow on my steps, a born survivor in any kind of clime.

After much showing of passports and clambering after donkeys, we arrived to no particular fanfare and settled in. We noticed the reverential attention given our passports simply because they were book-like. The red and white pasta pursued us most of the way, and we thanked our stars we had bestowed our lucky apartment on two such worthies as our newfound friend Hans, both jovial and sensitive, and his introverted *amie* Tabitha. Their collection of cut glass was everywhere, open to the world, a triumph of the glazier's art.

And now we were a universe away, it seemed, in a bed and breakfast, taking our ease at last in a stereopticon land of jute mountains and crags. Light's monstrous body, which dispossessed any sleeping arrangements in a huge dictatorial way, occupied much of the bed, though he was not in the least arrogant about this and apologized profusely, as he had been accustomed to doing all his life, especially to women. Always too long for anything, he suffered from cold feet despite the addition of many pairs of socks. I, on the other hand, was comfy and nearly nodding off when he started to talk.

"Nice bunch of folks."
"If you like their way of giggling."
"Give them a break."
"If you must."
"What are we here for?"
"Who knows?" I had forgotten.
"To see if we could do it."
"Just that." I was anxious for sleep.
"Surely not."
"Then what on earth?"

In our more serious, refined moments we occupied ourselves with the cosmic problems of the planet, particularly whether we were alone amid the millions of galaxies which had not once managed to sniff out a rival.

"So why haven't they said hello?"

"Oh," I countered, "we're not very appealing. Constantly at war. There aren't any UFOs forever laying siege to our skies—leave it at that."

"To have gotten here and not made the final step?"

"Why not? They could not bring themselves to do it, considering all the millions they'd sacrificed. They content themselves with observing us at our juvenile antics."

"Whereas *I* believe in them not at all. Wherever you look there's a dead cosmos."

"Impossible."

"UFOs non-existing."

"If you see it that way."

"I do. We are alone among everything."

"Sez you."

"Sez me."

"Goodnight to you."

It was not to be. I was wide awake and too alert (or too alerted) for this hegemony of barren salutations. My fingers ached, my spine felt jolted out of shape, and my head began a slight migraine that threatened to grow as the Outer Mongolia blues set in for a trumpery night of it.

As my woes increased, threatened by a sleep which would not come, I began in my formulaic way to rehearse once again what was wrong with our slice of universe. To begin with, why had all these UFOs—in which I believed, whose strange voyagers I desired to meet, had parleyed with in dreams, and could have summoned with the sheer magnetic force of my longing (a turbine that whirred inside me whenever I thought of them, as if they alone could heal my life)—why had they never declared themselves? Too finicky? Too exquisite? Used to better fare, fare less bloodthirsty or simple? What was the sticking point they all stuck at, where they dug in their prehensile toes (if they had toes), some of them, mind you, flitting near the 747s or 777s, their colors a fanfaronade of exotic lures, their steeples clearly visible, a montage of barrel rolling illuminations, almost teasing, welcoming, inviting us to follow.

Why then so standoffish? It was a fool's game perhaps, a mug or a mugwump's antic exemplifying in our very own language, *Come see us waggle our latest sneerd* or *come and touch the newest hornswoggle.* Call it what you will: a fragment of the unique, where all was pale and familiar. But no: I had never heard so much as a crackle, not a swoosh, not a whistle, not a rush of burly energy.

They crept upon us, an unpredictable visual sonata, never to go beyond into cacophony or whisper, staying surreptitious yet blatant, all with the same inaudible taste, whatever their shape. Not one risking a "How're you today?" or a banshee yell.

Talk they no doubt had on board aplenty, but we heard none of it, only enforced silence. Maybe we were, as a species, beneath contempt? Then why such a surfeit of interest in us? I was convinced that the interior of most spaceships was a bouquet of tones, with each Alien specially equipped to hear bleats from a dozen simultaneous sources.

Or were all the visiting spacefarers tone-deaf, and sound something they weren't privy to? If so, alas for them, they were a race of the dead if they couldn't hear our poetry from Homer to Crabbe.

Not a bit of it. That was no way to go. Thousands of deaf men (or whatever) playing consequences with a whole planet of jabberers. One Alien spokesman surely would have sufficed, for me, anyway. It made no difference really: a million versus one solitary eavesdropper. My mind perked up, as it usually did after a few moments of Alien reverie.

Whatever they used as a means of communication they did not use words: maybe something else filled in the gap. So why not send one arbiter just to clinch the point about human speech? What use was a thousand, a million aerial stalkers?

I ascribed this lapse to my semi-comatose condition and pushed on further to the hypothesis that read: *No human has yet made speech worth hearing.*

It was outrageous, so to dismiss the whole of speech in this way, but it could be the truth. A bevy of Alien nations so advanced that nothing had been said on Earth that was worth attending to. Even though they had been auscultating us since the Middle Ages, ever expectant, always disappointed. Why had the Aliens not gone elsewhere? Why persist with humanity? Vain hope. Vain longing.

Perhaps, I mused, getting bolder in my presumption, they chose us by default, there being nowhere else to go! Of all the available planets in the galaxy, this was the only one to sponsor life, highly unsatisfactory life, but the only taker. One day we might explode in worthy speech, but not yet, and they waited forever for the jubilant day to arrive, waited since the Middle Ages, the Dark Ages, and beyond.

Somehow this point emerged from my ashamed brain: somewhere, surely, a golden speaker flourished, a being whose every word was their kind of poetry. *That* was why the search for him became so intense, so desperate. They could have been crying for the moon—obviously no such speaker crept over the horizon. This was the best any of us could do, no matter how advanced we became in electronic sophistication, no matter how our speech mutated with time. None of it was ever good enough for them, that was it, and all the time we thought we were improving, getting better at it, trapped without knowing why, as if in the long-necked horse of a Peruvian sea monster, or in the bowels of that species of shark that gobbles its young as soon as born (Why were they not extinct long ago?). A life that does not lead anywhere, that was what we had saddled ourselves with. Not, that is, that we expected the Alien to come down, shake our hands, and utter the plaintive phrase: "We have been waiting so long for you." Or better: "It's been the merest smidge of time since we first left. Congratulations on your achieving regular speech."

With that, my traveling companion awoke, stirred perhaps by some petty allusion, to interfere or interrupt—I had whiled the night away with my madcap musings, all attitude and partly logical, but questionable.

Light Lomax said, "What's new?" with an old couldn't-care-less attitude, and after a pause I began telling him.

"Has it occurred to you," he replied, "that each and every UFO may be assigned a different speaker? To track him and record everything he says? The best of men can be quite original in their thoughts, brilliant even. The best of men are always brilliant. You want to catch all they say."

He smiled the smile of intuitive derision (a geek smile, as befits his profession) and patted my knee. "Don't take it so hard. These UFOs will get you down if you let them. Some things in life just can't be reckoned with, so you'd better not trouble your head with them."

I asked myself if I'd any right to adopt such a hedonistic *sang-froid* philosophy, decided that I would not, and started immediately on the same track as before: "How then do you account for people spotting them in numbers, tens of thousands? Answer me that, will you?"

His refreshed spirits met my crushed ones without answering even with shrug or grimace. Instead, he produced a phrase which had nothing to do with anything: "Tiger Leaping Gorge", though I had heard him exclaim something like it before. He then sketched on a convenient piece of khaki paper something like an assortment of potatoes, which went begging until he had finished and I asked in my sleepless, rude way: "So?"

Light explained that he had drawn, as best he could, the shapes of the UFOs he'd heard people had seen. I produce them here much as they were, though no amount of my handiwork could exactly copy their dubious shapes.

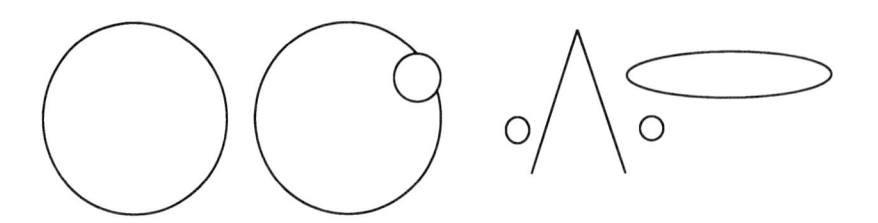

And so forth. I'd experienced much the same myself, apart from the close inspection-tour vouchsafed me a dozen years ago as I swam in the summer heat and saw this:

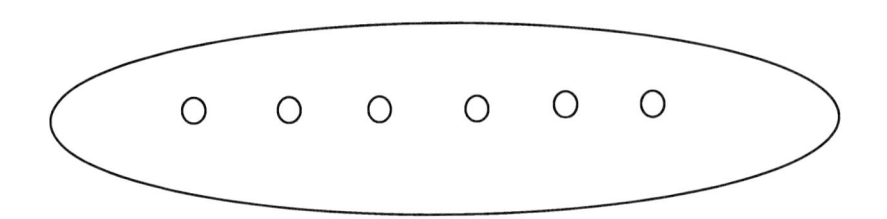

It had lingered for half an hour, silent, motionless, and then rocketed off at appalling speed, a dun thing, gleaming huge and letterless, like an insult in the sun, defying you to make sense of it while it lasted. He nodded as if it was all too familiar instead of being all too strange. Finally he said, "Twenty or thirty different kinds of shapes, some obscure. Some as plain as day. *Cui bono.*"

This habit of breaking into Italian irritated me, but I had enough Italian to cope with it. "What use," I said in echo. "What use is that?"

"A signal," he answered.

"A portent. If you like."

"Of things to come?"

"A Wellesian conceit, then."

"If you go that far." He was getting snide, or was I imagining it?

"A token of national pride."

"If you must."

"Saying, one day soon." I vowed to tease him further.

"You're some optimist."

"Why?"

"We haven't got the first flaming idea of whatever they are."

Then I ran past him the sum of all my sleepless agitation, finishing with, "Perhaps they intend nothing at all. They may all be empty."

"I thought you said they had propulsive power."

"They do. It's all robotic, though."

"How so?"

"There's nobody inside it."

"Nobody?"

"Empty vessels all. These envoys have no beings. All mechanical."

"You speak firsthand, having known them."

"I speak in true ignorance, Lomax, my friend. Can you do better?"

At last I fell asleep, dismissing all rational thought on the issue. When I awoke, after several hours of fitful slumber, it was with a profound sense of things minutely shrunken, just beyond a comfortable range of viewing. This phenomenon, not *always* reliable, was ever so gently propelling objects beyond visibility—telephone books, newspapers, sewing needles. I was going home, I told myself, going downhill among the lost teeth of the sharks.

What cheered me, just fractionally, was my lambent fascination with UFOs, which grew in majesty as I declined. I saw them as far back as the twelfth century, always the same long-lived observers, waiting for life on earth to become less violent. Waiting in vain, as it turned out, but waiting patiently all the same. Traveling as the mood seized them at the speed of light, they changed areas at insane pace, never discovering sane behavior among the humans below who were always game for another atrocity, another war, another "bloodless" coup, with fatalities mounding day after day. Most were even willing to overlook the killing at Darfur, for instance, because no one knew where it was, or how important Hutu-versus-Tutsi had become. But the UFOs noticed everything, and I wondered why they did not pack up and seek another planet. To which perhaps the answer was: all planets are the same, right to the end of their reign. It's possible that there had been, so far, no planet with safe goings-on, and the UFOs were waiting for all the warmongering to end. *That* was why they were never heard from. Theirs was a waiting game to beat all, a superlative nonstarter on who knows how many planets. In this scenario, their explorers' only reprieve was death among the surviving mollusks (or whatever), in perpetual submission, doomed forever to a silent, aberrant dark.

How presumptuous of me to purloin and imagine the lives of the UFOs, tamping them down and daring to know things about them unknown to other humans. It was a *chutzpah* I took pride in, and, like the Aliens, I was just waiting, having an eternity to waste. So unlike a former acquaintance of mine who, after devoting his lot to an undistinguished cause, found himself condemned in a one-line biography restricted to his height, after all that toil. Which found him shorter still.

TWO

Murmuring something about ice cream, Light Lomax went outside to taste the already half-spent day. Dimly, I began to return to my theme of the night before, barbarously calculating the odds of a universe divided by the sum total of UFOs, with neither quantity known nor even guessable. It was hopeless, and surely worth abandoning, but I relished dividing the odds by three: planets a swarm with life, planets where life no longer flourished, and planets inhospitable as bleached arid stars.

Strangely, it brought me a measure of self-esteem thus to divide things off. Something semi-precise where all was moving. Why so grateful, all of a sudden, for this piece of sublunary choplogic? I wrote it off as padding about in the deep throes of the universe for too long. It was the acme of mental fatigue, when the overtaxed brain gave up and cried for Momma to remove the impossible conundrum of the previous night. Yet part of me, the disobedient side, liked fondling the universe in this way, doomed to solve nothing but yet intoxicated to mingle with the grand unknowables for half-an-hour before mental fatigue set in and the thrill of discovering anything lapsed into the old ignorance of before.

Try for half an hour, I thought, and then cancel. Why does it thrill me to waste time in this way? A mental itch, it all came back to the same insoluble: *Why in the entire history of mankind had the UFOs not been heard from even once?* Boredom? Contempt? Bloody-mindedness? Massive patience? With what? Why persist with it further? Nothing else to do? Here my mind stopped. *Nothing else to do?* Strange to say, my mind may just have solved the enigma. Was it really the *Eureka* of the whole thing? In the tradition of hurry up and wait forever? Time must have a stop after all. If so, why not this one? For an instant all thoughts of waiting for something vanished, replaced by an opaque ether, and *oh* the relief I felt thus to fall asleep with *nothing* to wake up for. Or to. Then it was gone. The old obligation to make sense of things returned with a vengeance, and I settled down to work on the impossible all over again, passionate to construct something where all was nothingness.

Five decades of this fol-de-rol had brought me nowhere, apart from the usual tokens of the trade, D. Litts, and other medals, but little else of what truly mattered. My mind gazed back to the old notion of *nothing else to do,* noting how ungraspable the concept was, except that in this case the emphasis was on *nothing else,* invoking a mass of discarded butterflies not worth chasing. My mind gave thanks for something to desire.

Still and all, the concept of nothing haunted me, the very notion of a universe so vast and yet so—*untouchable.* And if not, *so blank. Something missing,* I thought, my mind invaded by preposterous sudden thoughts of one life-teeming Earth among so many millions of suns. Only one, and look how much of a mess we had made of that. If this were all, creation was a dismal failure and worth keeping silent about from beginning to end. I paused in my quest and for once tasted the silence of things, the hiss of blank creation.

In a dream, I fudged up some breakfast (a couple of slices of rye bread and some antique cheese) to make who knew what impact on my stomach. Both rye and cheese had traveled with me all the way from Manhattan and I assumed Light Lomax had fared better leaving food to the mercies of the locals.

In one sense, I *could* go home again. I need not have come at all, or only halfway; it was not a matter of distance traveled so much as an impulse from the brain within. No, in truth, I had been obliged to travel to find that particular impulse to begin with. None of this cooled my unquenched Alien ardor. I waited for Light Lomax to return.

"How many of them have *you* seen?"

"None. How many have you?"

"*One*, for half an hour."

"Poor odds. Some have seen them daily," commented Light, "all different. Those are the people you should be talking to."

"Drop the whole matter then."

"Do you really want to discuss it?"

"No. I can see you're not in the mood."

"Mood has nothing to do with it. You've not assembled the evidence."

"By my own lights, I have. Screw your evidence."

"Screw yours."

We had reached an impasse, not for the first time, and there was nothing to be done about it. I was adamant, Light Lomax was intractable. Perhaps, having come this far, we should have separated, never to speak again. Darwin and Christ had met, more or less, and disagreed. It was not the outcome I had been waiting for and neither of us would yield.

I thought back to my one personal UFO, its vast body turned toward me, like a giant of the sky arrived to consult one of the local astronomers. Rounded windows, pointed nose, no sound, its color a muted beige. How vivid, how resplendent. No sign of occupants. No movement. Then it had flown sideways, up and away, at incalculable speed. Never seen again, although dozens of friendlies had seen something similar and marveled. This was *my* UFO, by unnatural right, watching me, playing the waiting game.

On another front, during our vigil in Mongolia, there had been the willingness of the local women to make use of their bodies, as if we were visiting tax inspectors or pedigree-obsessed mountebanks. Jolly, roly-poly, olive-skinned and of a fearsome body odor, these doxies rolled in the hay with us to our heart's content, obliging us this way and that with incongruous naiveté. We might have been a herd of horses or a convocation of orangutans for all the difference our human status made to them. To them we were as homunculi, fit for service, but nothing else, a species of local stag ripe for plucking now and then.

We drifted along with what they put on offer, dreading the day when the shutters went down and the doxies turned their attentions elsewhere. We became used to their perfunctory, absent-minded caresses, making of us draft animals with better things to think about.

Astonishing, really, this rough-and-ready sexuality contrasted with the high-strung desire and speculations we busied our minds with—despite the fundamental disagreement that divided us. There was something that bound our feeble clips to that sublunary desire. The smell of the byre, maybe, or the smell of an often poked finger into that or this aperture.

These ladies knew everything and found it boring and their constant silence during our times together only made them more ferocious, as if the pair of us were neighbor automatons, out for a spree. We plugged on, we plugged in, forgetting we were born to be disappointed and tucked in among other human corpses in the end.

So time passed in its funereal way, between tupping and astronomy, neither getting us very far except for my abiding—although recently arrived at—conviction that the UFOs were waiting us out, eyes in the sky since the dark, Dark Ages. I could see myself among them, a successor to Clyde Tombaugh, the discoverer of Pluto, who once had languished by his lens until his soul ached and the lovely hunk of rock swam into view, seen (by humans at least) for the first time.

What I would later call a brain wave (of the sort I had had since childhood) afflicted me. This migraine, as the complaint was called, began with an eye dazzle that affected sight, and sometimes abolished it. Attacks could last a few minutes or some days (in my case a few hours at least), followed by the classic thumping headache. After virtually a lifetime of suffering, I discovered that a bag of frozen peas compressed against the offending blur would bring relief in five minutes, god alone knows why. This left a space between the attack at its worst and the relief thus procured. But sometimes I actually prolonged the sequence, curious where it might lead. Usually it produced a deck of blanks, and seeing through things instead of seeing them plain.

This had long amused me, until the experience became too extreme. I marveled at the falsity of the system: I could not see what I could, and therefore could see what I could not. In truth, I saw both simultaneously—so long as I could endure its vagaries before the excruciating pain began—delighting in the triumph of light, my very own crown filled with stars as if by royal proxy. The memory of a migraine persisted long after it had fled, memories of ascending into the quite unseizable domain of the black hole, where diurnal life consisted of cats, roebucks, and humans alike stretched thin as linguini. After which there was much time left to obsess, to posit a brutal relapse into pain.

Note: did the agony that followed match the ripe golden moments of the previous sensation? Hardly, but I persisted in making them equal, stealing from the zone of agony the half-inch of suave delight it offered me, trusting lifelong the quizzical gods of migraine to see me through. At any rate, this was my experience of heaven, conspired at, partly yielding, never conquered quite, but tempting always with the fruits of frankincense and myrrh, before the gates of hell opened and all expressions of delight foundered amidst a scream of a kitten stretched out on the black hole machine.

The Aliens were migraine sufferers—this was their true condition. I was positive. Not unlike other creatures in this world, they emerged half-made. By the time they reached full agility, maybe the human animal would have sobered up. This was why the Aliens rode the world in blameless ignorance. A matter of timing, with one life form second-guessing the other, neither side as yet appeased.

A skiing accident put paid to Light, at least for six months, during which I remained in place among the Outer Mongolians, whose quantum of wantum seemed to have fallen off the charts. Maybe it was the absence of my erstwhile friend, whose lusts outpaced mine. I kept to myself the discovery that I had made about the Aliens all suffering from migraine bouts, maybe even undergoing a permanent affliction which no human could remedy. But still hungering for them to touch me, send me a bone-shivering flare.

Until then, I would keep my station, a quiet, expectant life sustained by doses of the hand-to-mouth gruel (*mistmurk*) which was the locals' staple food. Each waking day I would pause for the first sound of the Aliens' long-delayed funereal patter, calling me out of hiding to experience the sublime chatter of their children, so long annulled and choked, and the never-before-heard cacophony of their blessed hosannas of triumph.

Ah, I wished with all my heart (missing a beat or two now and then and speeding with inexplicable consequences) for a migraine-free reprieve for all of them, no more bone-racking skull pain or miserable quinsy of peering to decide what is not there. I longed for reprieve, for them, for me, in a world of cockahoop whimsy with a brain free to improvise, despite the bleeding furnace of feelings, our hearts chiming in consonance, nary a heartbeat missed nor aorta out of place.

In short, I yearned for a world intact, for them, for me, a cosmos where all fitted in, no disappointments, no aggrieved complaints, a world where every lamb had its day, roly-poly in fresh abandon, with places reserved for even the vilest nightmare. If I only wished hard enough, I thought, things would keep coming together as they were destined to do, and the Aliens would step down kindly, in a rush of willing accommodation to greet this other Alien in a spaceship of his own. I wished until my blood ran hot again, trying to master creation while there was yet time, before the voyagers left, before we were all ground to cinders.

THREE

I hesitate to call it sleep. Rather it was fitful and traumatic, a *mélange* of unseized childhood opportunities, a girl unkissed and long ago surrendered to the workday world, or another (older) whom I dared not touch beyond a certain point for reasons of mesmeric distinction—bad breath or something deeper, maybe a wealth of erotic experience beyond my twelve years. Then there was the plentiful supply of girls who ran through the procedure in a demented hurry. Hurry on to the next. These were too ready, only too willing, and (when I had time to think) impetuously sensual. They frightened me with their casual technique, their willingness to try anything. One or two girls, however, made serious overtures, not hasty nor perfunctory. They seemed born for it, and perhaps were, sensing my diffidence and curing it. These were the girls I remembered most in my eyrie up there in the dusty plains, particularly the Italian one who said, in almost a feral-growl, as if I had invented such a caress, *ti a quoque,* meaning do to me what I did to you—whatever that was—my Italian wasn't equal to it, and she never explained. Presumably I managed to do it, unknowingly, and she moved on to more agile workmen.

But the sound of it—*ti a quoque*—came back to me over the years and made me wonder at what I had evidently done, slipped into her bouquet of erotic memoirs along with all the others, some bad, some passable, some heaven-sent. She, if she survived, was an old hag by now, harassed by grown children and weary of it all. Yet she survived in her Italian way, blithe and buxom, buoyant and bold, calm in her expectation of being pleasured. Oddly enough, she brought the Alien migraineurs and a *ti quoque* close together in my mind. If the enforced silence of the migraineurs was a bit of wishful thinking, as it was (arrived at in desperation), so was the flummoxed adolescence of those boyhood years, guessing at nirvana. In either case, it was a matter of not knowing how. Was I missing Light Lomax? Not a bit of it. I was wishing myself more alert in imagining the impossible.

I forced my addled brain to concentrate, dimly aware that I was making a poor job with the UFOs. Migraineurs all? It didn't make a hell of a lot of sense, and I could see why. At least half of them were not migraineurs at all, but lively chatterers, alert and vocal. The other half might have been silent, variety being the spice of life. But all being migraineurs didn't add up, not when you were dealing with an advanced civilization that flew at the speed of light (and maybe beyond), to the dismay of earthlings.

My notion of migraineurs was a stopgap, a convenient bit of goods until some better idea turned up. It was easy to say, but impossible to perform. OK: no more migraine sufferers. What then? A whole regiment of Aliens keeping mum in the absence of anything interesting going on? It beggared belief. Or the talking part was handled by mammoth UFOs that circled the firmament relentlessly, macro-mammas to the micro, especially skilled at addressing earthlings? If so, why had none of them spoken up? What was holding them back? Perhaps, I fantasized, none of this crew would speak to *me,* saving eons of illustrious commentary for someone worthier. To everyone else they chattered to beat the band, inexhaustible and lucid.

I soon scotched that unlikely theory and fixed my gaze on what really counted: the quality of their silence. Could our UFOs be like the elephants, inaudible but speaking volumes out of human reach? What was the point when they had been sent to eavesdrop upon us and our miscreant doings?

It was simple: they were reporting back to base in their own language, which outpaced human speech in all ways—a fetching language, with all kinds of jumbo speak, remote from human purview just because our hearing did not extend that far. In the distant future, maybe it would, enriching our world with a kaleidoscopic dialect making us scoff at the paltry voices of my generation.

It was a plausible theory. Why then maintain my suspicion of it? Perhaps it was not simple enough to satisfy Occam's razor and all that ancient palaver. I had heard of beings, secreted in the bowels of the sea, that wriggled or swam where nothing had the right to be, down in the extremest trenches of being. Surely, with such an extreme marine example, a UFO was entitled to have a singularity of its own, a voice elephantine, coelacanth, or dolphin. I had been laboring under an old delusion, ethnocentric as blazes, relegating the unknown world to nonexistence merely to satisfy a need for balance.

From now on, I vowed, my life would be full of the unexplained, unknown, and enigmatic. I would no longer complain about the silence of the UFOs, but take it on the chin, convinced that one day, soon or distant, all would be available to us, even the creatures of the deepest seas. It might have been the beginning of a religious view, in which I became one of those mystics who supped with holy rats, both equal parts of the same cosmos.

Why then did I second-guess myself, believing and not believing, anxious to reject the fertile muddle? I wrote the needs of men off to human velleity, yielding to the old slogan of "I want it, I want it now." That was the commonplace human in me, shy of postponing things, and coming up with the indefensible notion of instant gratification. If not now, *never*. I labored mightily to resist all such thoughts, knowing how fast things mutate (typewriter to computer), but could not gainsay the supersti-

The Invisible Riviera

tious part of my mind that whispered: the UFOs will speak *now*—or never.

I began to detect the first glimmerings of madness in my behavior. Not a bad way to go, I reassured myself, at least that will cut out the worry. Some anyway. Equivalent to having a refined posterior notch, which I have had lifelong, though never obsessing myself about it. Just another glitch in the system, to be followed by others no doubt, as the housing eroded and collapsed with mounting age. Why worry? I'd already done enough of that, and hoped for an end to it.

I still had transitional worries, like the inability to read the calendar, to say exactly which day was which, and my neighbors were of no help, basing their lives on a calendar I did not read. To hell with time-schemes I thought—I have enough troubles already with the timeline of the UFOs.

And so it went, one side of my mind dismissing the calendar and all such frippery, the other side perpetually recovering the Aliens, even though I had dismissed them too. You are witnessing, I told myself, the birth of an obsession, the rebirth of an obsession momentarily banned, but there for the rest of my days unless something world-shattering happened. Again and again I reviewed the alternatives: migraine, dumbness, indifference, elephant-talk, and so on. And it made no difference.

The cause eluded me. I recalled in loving detail the incident of years ago when the huge shape parked at two thousand feet or so, and lingered for easily half-an-hour: silent, vivid, and serene, with nobody looking out of its windows (that I could see)—and eventually clearing out at impossible speed. Had I missed something the apparition seemed to be telling me? Had I been someone else, would he have seen it in a flash and reported it? I kept my silence for years, and still do, waiting perhaps for some corroboration, a word to the wise.

Well, I had not advanced one jot, and it threatened to go on like that until the end of time. So, no wonder I intermittently backslid and resurrected the old impossibilities, hoping one would yield, especially the one in which the Aliens were waiting for our world to end before taking over—the result not of some cataclysmic bomb blast extinguishing all human life, but of, say, the hordes of Muslims overpowering the Christians and the Jews, and both sides abolishing themselves even though their infrastructures remained more or less intact, ready for the next occupants. Such was my nightmare-laced pipe dream of the future, my horrific takeover myth.

Perhaps if I had restricted my doings, my obsessions, to Inner Mongolia rather than Outer, things would not have reached this panic point. I missed Light Lomax, my erstwhile traveling companion and was bold enough to address him, over the countless miles, in the directest way possible, by trusty computer, miniaturized according to some sleek, young, child-geek's dream, lightning-fast:

> Sir, you are missed. This not to minimize the extent of your injuries, but to persuade them to mend. Any word from you would be appreciated. Even if from the depths of despair. My concern with the UFOs is driving me mad: there is not there, if you get my meaning. Nothing to chop at, nothing even to complain about if not the absence of any signal or sign from them. Does the universe not care about the impression it's making?
>
> Yours,
> Karl

That should spirit him out of his foxhole, I thought, recalling the old days of long-leggedness and women lusting for our bodies. If he didn't reply, then I was none the worse for asking. If he did, then I'd be glad I sent up an electronic smoke signal.

A few hours later, as the milky sun set, came his reply. Somehow he had made my act of reading it as painful as his two broken legs, even though the typed response was word-perfect, properly organized, and pithy. It read:

Know that I am crippled beyond belief. Fucking snow. Tabitha is looking after me. Bad sprain to my left arm. Concussion still a source of helpless agitation. Can't actually move for six months, and even then...I see you are keeping the home fires burning out there among the natives. Give my love to the doxies. And to you my abiding envy.

Light

In other words, stay off my land. He didn't want to be bothered with my juvenile antics. Not a word re: UFOs, but that was typical of him. Confide in him the thing that's driving you mad, and he would write about anything but.

I cooled down after my initial burst of anger. (I should have known.) There he sat, living the life of Riley, comfortable and warm, with Tabitha looking after his every need. Lithe Lomax, brother to men and a haven to women, victim of a snowball accident.

It was up to me to provide my own entertainment—doxies, UFOs, and whatever else I could fudge up. I was a man on my own in foreign country, an outcast hating all men for their malevolent narcissism. Like one to the manor born, I resolved to beat the denizens of the UFOs on my own turf.

After a few moments' cognition, I hot-flashed him a message all the way around the world, in reply.

"What about the UFOs? Surely there's enough evidence to persuade an unbeliever like you?"

Half an hour it took. Probably arousing him from a deep sleep—no, the message was silent. He was awake in his orthopedic misery.

"So what?"

It went on in this vein for quite a while; my chiding him, he exploding time and again, but both unable to leave the damned machines alone.

My message ran, "Don't be a spoiler."

His was predictable, "Spoil what? I have two broken legs."

I will spare you the rest. Suffice to say that it was full of mounting impatience, my irritability feeding on his rich indifference. The farther a friend is from you, the less you feel his pain, or at least you shove it into some optional slot, to be attended to later. Or not at all. The more I hounded him about UFOs, the more he bitched about his legs. On the other hand, he seemed glad to hear from me. This I could tell from the infrequent intervals when I got off the point and referred him to the doxies, the strange obsession of the locals with books, or the changing seasons, ranging from dust storm to snow.

After several hours of this fol-de-rol, he desisted, signed off, asking me as a parting shot why I didn't send the Aliens packing and invent some other line of interest. Or break a leg, which would give me something real to think about. At that, I ceased the chat with him by flicking a small switch.

My thoughts turned to space again, not the horizontal version but the vertical. Were they different? The one deliquesced into the other, but with more space to roam into, the troposphere versus the atmosphere. Consider the wealth of stars surrounding us up there, the regions patrolled at inhuman speed by the Aliens and their parent star systems. The trouble was that we were dealing with the Aliens at close quarters, where they should have had something to say—the racing results, the chance of being bombed by the Iranians, the poetry of Crabbe and Keats. And so forth. Were they just waiting us out, the old babble forgotten just when the new felt free to begin after so long a wait?

Sometimes a pernicious thought dogged my progress through the frigid afternoons as I said my *sain bainuus's* (hello) to the waiting locals, who then left me alone to meditate what secret thing I meditated on. The terrible thought was that Aliens simply did not exist, were a hoax invented by fly-by-night visionaries. And the thousands of UFOs, so called, were creatures not even of conjectural substance, sent to plague us and ultimately lose heart. This had been, was, Lomax's version, dismissing his four visual sightings as mere will-o-the-wisps, a child's fairy tale for his slack moments. Even if he had feigned to see them, all delineated in their various shapes (which intrigued me no end, they looked so convincing), he had not seen them at all and was doing it just to humor me as one long lost to rational speculation. I was the ghastly phantom at my own opera, lost amid the other ghosts, a near goner if you asked him, retrievable only for sex and meals.

I cherished the illusion, but each time only for the shortest period, imagining how much easier my life would be *sans* UFOs. Not to worry about them any more, especially about the soundlessness of their performance. I had seen one—large as life—and that presumably was my ration. I even then dawdled them out of existence only to bring them back, belatedly recognizing that the plural was forbidden, me who had seen only one. They were not life, they were not death, but somehow in between, scarecrows of the fifth dimension sent to worry us to get on with our wars so that the Aliens could take their ease.

Any chimera would do, I thought. Anything to clear up the latifundia so the Aliens could move in, and eventually repopulate the Earth by thousands and millions: The Peaceful People, as they would be known. The permanent ones, the ones destined to prevail over their rough and ready forbears (us).

At other times, I believed in them with all my heart, if you discount my wobbling about their sound. That would take care of itself, I persuaded myself, and I tried to look the other way, deluding myself, perhaps, but convinced in my heart of hearts that this would come to pass. If I could only hear the sounds of it. No, I was not promised a rose garden, far from it, but I could hope, maybe with my dying breath, to hear the first sound of Alien confabulation, summing up the weather or the stench of dead humans awaiting cleanup.

This was the kind of incertitude I practiced during my middle period (the period without Lomax). As the locals said, "It's peaceful" (*tai-van bain*). Sometimes too much so.

I longed for some palatable food, not the greasy lamb favored by Mongolians, but some bacon and eggs, in my case refined into Smart Bacon (no fat) and EggBeaters (no cholesterol). But no hope of the latter, too exquisite and jejune for experienced Mongol tastes. I soldiered through, but noticed my fat consumption had gone up. I would have been better off patronizing the Chinese restaurants of Ulan Bator, but I stayed put (for the time being), concentrating on tea based on a milky drink served in wooden jugs, and fried mutton fat or fried flour. These people had found a use for mutton fat!

No use complaining when you cannot speak the language. You are lucky to have something to chew on. On special occasions the whole sheep would be gutted, and the chief guest invited to carve. Left over meat could often be found on the roof poles. When a sheep was slaughtered, the deed was done by making an incision close to the heart and pinching it down.

These instructions for an Ulan Bator orgy are hard to bear, but the resultant four ribs of lamb are good enough to get through to the next bacon and egg (I wish). My own preference, after repeated lamb, would be for *solar moss*, a thing lurking in the shady side of solar prominences, a new discovery which made me wonder how anything on the sun could be thought shady.

The longer I stayed there, the more bizarre the practices back home seemed, and the more natural the local way of behaving with milk or lamb became. Down south there was the Gobi Desert to contemplate, with signs of human habitation becoming fewer and fewer; once past Tokham, you were really into it, the land of powdery earth blown into your eyes and of always carrying your own food. The short way into China beckoned you, and I did all I could to resist. Due south of Ulan there was the 300,000 year-old skeleton, and I hoped that finding it would not reflect my own future, bleak though it seemed. Perhaps I would succumb to the charms of Ulan Bator year after year. Maybe Lomax would come and rejoin me after regrouping his knees. Perhaps, though, this was all pipe dreamery. *No one will come*, I thought, *I will be alone*, waiting for the break that never comes, the end of the world and the consequent beginning of UFO-dom. I made a list of things to do:

>   Learn the language at last.
>   Decline to attend the funeral of Light Lomax, should he die.
>   Visit the rumored birthplace of Ghengis Khan, due east of here.
>   Become a permanent resident of the Ulan Bator Post Office, waiting for mail or rain.

I returned to the present day, reminding myself to take my daily dose of the anti-inflammatory, Mobic, which I nicknamed Moby-Dick. The pain in my knee was growing monsoon-like, and soon there would be two of us *hors de combat*.

Returning to my now almost constant obsession, I soon dismissed all thoughts of the Aliens not existing. There was too much evidence for that. The real question was: why not trumpet it on the White House lawn? Were they dumb, deaf (a weaker case), or just bloody choosy, having found no one anywhere, who met their impossible standards? Why, in the broadest trance of their vocal skills, had they spoken (so the myth went) to the Tom, Dicks, and Harries of our so-called civilization? Instead of, say, Carl Sagan, Frank Drake, Enrico Fermi, and the rest of their tribe? A chat with the luminaries would do a world of good. Why not address themselves to the *honnête hommes* of our reputed world, Edith Cavell, Mother Theresa, Gandhi? Why not these masters of probity and the saint of rectitude?

A worthy idea? Absolutely. Why then had they not done it years ago when these gentlemen and ladies were fresh meat, presuming the UFOs were functioning at the time? This always stopped me, the rationalist balked by the enigma, the kind heart (more or less) thwarted by estoppel. Perhaps I was just the wrong person to deal with. Someone else could have taken over and accepted the first critique: *Why fight one another when there are butterflies?*

Thousands, of course, had had similar thoughts, some of them more judiciously spaced then mine. Why, I asked, must the abductees remember the carpenter's drill, the eyeball macerations, the embryo plucked out of the body cavity, *and not remember a word that got said?*

Why so silent in the face of devastation? I did not believe in such travesties, yet I clung to my Aliens, knocking my head against their silence, but still determined to crack their carapace. What, then, I asked? The great day would arrive, the first locution ("Where are you now, young Lochinvar?"), and what then?

In fifty years they would, just like the vanished and vanquished earthlings, be at one another's throats, a horde of bloodthirsty masters of arts determined to get to the bottom of things and then push with all their might. Pardon my cynicisms, but I had bad dreams, even though I still believed in virtue. Would it honestly come to that? Another hardscrabbling race making compulsive war on its predecessor, letting the world go hang.

Such caterwauling thoughts never left my side. Again and again I racked my brain on the question of the UFOs and their strange behavior, a grudging revel, or, if not that, an overflowing crustiness. A halfway type of perfection, full of decisions not taken, love undeclared at the last moment. I fancied if I were to hit on the right combination of thought and will, all would be clear, and a current of Alien thought would begin to flow.

Occasionally, I found succor in novel, melodic words, notably *tesseract* and *hummingbird*, but more often sighed under the outbreak of neologisms imperfectly understood and relegated to the monkey-chatter of infidels. I mean *geek, spavined, firewall,* and hundreds more, which a few moments of cogitation would have made clear to me, but I demurred, thinking I had enough going on. One day soon, I saw myself introducing the Aliens to *my* language, and laughing with unfeigned delight as they advanced from one delighted discovery to the next. They would be quick studies, deftly able to skip from one language to another in their already teeming word-hoard. They would be willing students, in a trice bypassing the rest of us stumbling around in Earthspeak.

For now, I contented myself with their silence, convinced of the plenty to come. Which amounted to zip thus far, I reminded myself, falling with an invisible bruise onto the plane of harsh reality. Surely, in my silent, bleached mental whirl, if I were willing to concentrate, the infant sounds of their squirming pursuits could be heard. I tried, but nothing came through—not even the ghostly whir of their spaceships. Nothing to chew on, nothing to echo. I listened again, and found only the hiss of background radiation to humor me. Surely they could do better than that. But no, they held their breath valiantly, and it suddenly occurred to me that their vocal system might not be breath-driven at all, but some weird unvoiced inward plosion, at which they were supremely gifted. They would never be heard, long after they had supplanted us. And we, any of us left over, would train ourselves to enter the domain of the silent.

Fat chance, I grumbled. I was going nowhere fast, and exchanging one silent hoax for another, all of them barren and hopeless. Meanwhile, the unheard chatter of the Aliens knew no bounds, leaping from one mental rollercoaster to another, discovering the rudiments of earthling existence with unheard whoopees and strange insentient cuffs on the wrists. To be shut out of all this performative zeal was too much to bear, but no matter how hard I listened, nothing seeped through, not a whimper, not a whisper.

I soon came to earth again, glad of my doxies who communicated in a language equally baffling, but I could tell volumes as they threw to the eavesdropper an occasional squeal, guffaw, or hiss of intaken breath. They were superb.

The sleek plane, as if looking for a place to set down, made a few hesitant maneuvers, lunges rather than directed motions, settled on one untidy piece of turf, and landed awkwardly in full view of the observers. After some while a figure stepped out of the badly canted disk only to falter and claw the ground before lying prostrate a few feet from the ragged form of the craft.

The observers hung back at first, suspecting all was not well in the interior (awaiting a blast, which did not come). Then two or three of them advanced, feeling their way, realizing that the plane's trouble had started on final approach—heart attack in the pilot or severe malfunction of the ailerons—sufficient to make the landing hazardous. Clearly, there were other occupants, too maimed to get out. While one person attended to a wounded astronaut who lay comatose, others attempted to reboard the plane, first trying to find a means of access underneath. The rest of the crew seemed to be dead, except for his partner, lying writhing on the ground, making squeaking sounds and clearly in pain.

Slowly the observers' movements became less tentative, more probing, as they perused the dead crewmen and the wreckage of the small saucer-shaped plane, impressed by the virtual absence of controls.

Up drove a military vehicle and that ended the tour of the wreckage. Loudspeakers invaded the peace of the rural scene, commanding them to back away and leave the saucer and its two occupants to the men in khaki.

"Just when we were getting interested," was the comment. Nothing of the kind had ever happened before. A fortunate few had snapped up portions of fabric for later display, and soon the diminutive saucer was aboard the truck, all the traceable debris bumped into corners under the tarpaulin, and off went the makeshift convoy to a questionable destination.

Those left behind mulled over their fate, severed in the act of inquisitive charity, and inclined to resent all interrupters as creatures of the devil. Later, they would expose their booty to the eyes of other villagers, in peculiar fragments of tape bearing simple signs that baffled nonetheless, and samples of silver paper that straightened out again once creased. God only knew what they had missed there on the ground, filaments of cosmic radios perhaps or fragments of flying needles, and they occupied themselves forever after seeking to retrieve *something* of what beggared belief.

So goes the story. That was 1947, year of our Lord, by many forgotten but not by the fans of Roswell. For them, the mythos goes eternally, the live astronaut, the curious emblems, the bits of (plastic?) strewn around. Indeed, the fact of the UFOs being transported to Wright-Patterson base gave the myth more room to move about in, and sons of the original team of discoverers were full of their fathers' discoveries, which they glowingly reported with fresh combed hair and family pride, the ex-major substituted for by the second lieutenant's son.

Plus all the new fans, making Roswell into a pyrotechnical holy grail. Subsequent announcements, feeble as the stuff they were printed on, made light of the experience, fobbing it off as a balloon, nay a Russian balloon, but everyone knew a fake was a fake, whatever the Air Force said. And small boys and girls danced with delight at the prospect of having their own Roswell to celebrate. Roswell, either mythic or real, basked in a groundswell of speculative praise, for being the magical zone it was. Where angels (or their modern substitutes) had trod, giving the Earth new meat to devour, the first of the few (latecomers added Area 51 and imitations thereof).

Who could blame them, marooned in a culture where TV commercials chivvied them to report to the nearest doctor any erections lasting four hours or more, or jubilation on discovering the first Siberian weasel. A culture of the young. And the old as well. Coming together to rebuild a myth denied by the officials of copybook maxims: you have not seen what you think you saw. And anyone pretending to do so will be transported to the desert and abandoned.

Vain hope! The people would go on believing what they saw, plus anything that merited suspicion. And what better than a flying saucer forced into one's ken by a timid air force? So went my own belief, tempered as it was by the insecurity of trusting a popular myth. I could no more *prove* the existence of the Roswell story than I could the constant presence of the UFOs. I still believed, picking and choosing my myths, almost at random, clearing out the crucifixion, for example, but retaining Sodom and Gomorrah.

Call my effort an attempt to imitate the fashion or style of the Tipsy Coachman, who according to legal parlance gets things right for the wrong reason or valiantly produces good from bad. I think I am entitled to both. The thought occasionally crossed my mind that, just as there was no knowing why the Aliens were so silent, there was no knowing about death. Both were regions of non-discovery. Of course, I preferred the silence of Aliens to a universe of death.

In my haste to recover what brains I had left to me, I abandoned the Tipsy Coachman (promising to call on him again, later) and regained normality, by a devious route including several species of UFOs neglected in form and stature. Such as their silence, attributed to leglessness, though this would hardly explain their fully-fledged intellects. Such as their congenital dumbness, even though this had nothing to do with their intelligence. Such as their blindness, causing also their dumbness, even though this affected their intelligence not at all.

But these were *pis allers,* elementary devices geered for a profound problem. No good as hypotheticals, the last ditch efforts of a brain already fatigued. Low-grade attempts unworthy of someone of intellectual caliber. I tried to go forward with a more intelligent line of reasoning, but my brain resisted and sent me packing to the region of the brain dead. One day soon, I would crack the puzzle, no doubt finding it an object of consummate simplicity which, had I had my wits about me from the first, I would have solved in a trice, and spent the rest of my days in self-congratulation.

I could leave it at what I had deduced thus far (the Aliens deemed it not worth speaking to us until we improved). But no, that was too simple. The brain demanded a much more complex solution. More flexing of intellectual prowess; et cetera. So I was stuck, between a rock and a hard place, tempted to meditate on the Aliens' attitude to birth and death, if any. For all I knew, on Earth the Aliens could be eternal, which made hay of my suppositions about longevity among the species. For all I knew, each type of spaceship harbored a different stripe of Alien, from those eternal to those short-lived.

Such were my misgivings. I had heard rumors about the various types of spaceship, and my own meager experience totaled one seen versus a dozen read about. Why on earth assume they were all alike? The concept was fatuous. Some of my contemporaries even thought that one spaceship could contain creatures of all kinds, sent to earth to survey human physiognomy. A brave idea, not yet come to fruition. Meantime I, and several thousand others, were busy scratching our heads over a puzzle soluble by answering *They speak like elephants,* too deep in the bass notes to be heard. It was as simple as that.

I saw eternity the other night, wrapped gray. Which means I saw a fraction of it through the gray frame of my window, a rectangle of dim light punctuated by snow. How many starry dots there were: sixty thousand, give or take ten or fifteen thousand, and I thought how incredible it seemed that there wasn't at least one dot calling out to us across the light-years. And how many Aliens were signaling nonstop to no avail. No, I was dreaming again. The light from the stars was getting through, although not the sounds of UFOs.

It didn't make sense, at least until you reflected that even the smallest star, shining so stably through the back window, was a whopper, whereas planets were much fainter, and besides were of different ecological systems. It stood to reason that anyone dealing with a message from outer space could hardly be sure if it was planetary or a stellar. *Something* was coming through: only one thus far (*Wow*, the system screamed, never to be heard from again). Some renegade impulse was surely driving the nature of things, and I had begun to compare the silence of the visible stars to the silence of the UFOs, though differing in countless ways. Was there some unwritten edict saying if you cannot hear them though you can see them, it must be because they too can be seen but not heard? As I opened the glass, admitting cool air into the coziness of my burrow, all the stars stood out in silent splendor, and the second UFO of my life was nowhere to be seen.

Clearly the stars, if and when we reached them, would be sources of unimaginable fury, whereas the UFOs remained marooned in a permanent silence. My basic feeling was one of exclusion from everything. What had the synods of perfection got against communicating? If the result made sense to anyone, in whose world was it? A race not yet born, from whom the first thing to be mastered was cosmic esperanto?

I closed the window in a mood of lamentation, wondering how many more stargazers were sharing my displeasure. Perhaps the stars and the UFOs, despite the colossal divergence of their origins, were in league against us. Twin types of soundlessness, fit to drive us mad, a double whammy of sorts, both aimed at a generation as yet unborn. I opened the window, hoping to trap a fragment of sound, star or UFO, but no luck. I closed it and turned my thoughts inward, eventually dreaming of white rats in their haven of Karni Mata, India, and how natural it seemed to suck their spittle.

When I woke up, at least six hours later, my brain posed a different problem. If the black-body radiation (which assailed our ears from everywhere) was a permanent presence (as it was), why could we not hear other samples of it too? I had no idea, but vowed to investigate the matter if I ever escaped the clutch of doxiedom. Some of the local women had made threatening motions to me, and then had cascaded into hysterical laughter at my uneasiness. If only snowbound Lomax had been available to counter such threats with those long legs of his. But he was far away, no longer of service.

My thoughts returned to the inhospitality of the UFOs and the stars, doting on how lively our lives would be if only we could hear more of what was going on out there. Why was the universe so cheapskate with us? Why deny sound when you have already bypassed the speed of light, penetrated black holes, and solved some mysteries of ghastly human behavior?

Orai, I said, mistaking the word for morning, *I must eat something.* My blood sugar was dropping fast, so I produced some *toms* (potatoes) from my overworked locker and wolfed it down. Eaten raw, the *toms* had a putrid, wintry quality, but nothing would hold me back, and I had eaten such before, at least half a dozen times, without flinching from the bouquet. I wondered what the time in the States was, and achieved a rough approximation. Lomax was just going to bed, as best he could, and I felt a pang of bleak surrender as I thought of him there in his icebound fastness. He was nobler than I.

Going out to make water, I found myself distracted by an old photograph of war—with a *burst of color,* scarlet functioning for the first time in a war photograph of strangely clad warriors with pikes and spears. Circa 1915 or so.

Long after I finished, the picture absorbed me, tweaked as it was at eye level on a thumbtack. I plunked it down as if it would help me in what was to come, planting it next to a photograph of my mother and father, long gone (restored to any maker), he beginning to go bald in his 70s, she with russet hair, still not gray in her 90s. They together added up to 160 or more years. Amazing when you come to think of it, the pianist and the soldier; surviving that long through wars, pneumonia, and Stokes-Adams attacks—enough to send off any normal person. But these two continually returned to the fray, determined to prevail, come what may. How any soldier came up with a pianist to court is a different matter, maybe some retrograde motor impulse consecrated to finding the right key. Or the correct mode of saluting.

How did they get together, apart from being childhood sweethearts? I, unconvinced by that pious rectitude, fished down among the dead men for booty: How did they produce two children? What led up to this, my father disinclined because of the war, my mother all frigid tenderness, they too agreeing on the wholesale of sex as "that rubbish." They managed it nonetheless, twice, as if possessed by a golden or gilded interim, two cathartic souls committed to a sportive interlude, after which life could return to normal. I count my sister and myself as prodigies of the night, when sex could have its say, and then be put back among the unmentionables until a birth so clouded with alleluias it did not count as the result of a sex act at all.

This was my meditation while making water into the bright pisshole of the day. Meditation on a birth. *And what have you done with God's gift since then?* I thought. Not bad, I told Millie and Alf, not bad at all. *And what on earth are they doing now?*

A profitable occupation for a middle-aged man, an old man, a man even older? I had no answer, and even the standard retort of *I've tried everything else* rebounded with accusatory force. *Why bother with that, now?* The only thing left undone, I explained, the only other thing to do, to "get." I heard the sounds of Coleridge welcoming me among the shades with ribald entreaty: *I wish he would explain his explanation.*

I used to be so agile, so limber. I spend my time yawning like a chasm, best of all of it behind me, except one little puzzle.

I remembered my father vividly, all the way from his Calvary to his demob five years later. First, the news "flashed" to his parents: Killed in Action 1918. Second, he'd come round, blinded in both eyes, underneath a dead Tommy whose name was Blood and whose earthly remains deluged my father. Then the parade of wounded men en route to the aid station, one behind the other.

Then the year of blindness as they treated both eyes. Followed by the advent of the American surgeon Dr. Archibald McIndoe (sounds like a Canuck) who said, "I can save his right eye." Then a year of practicing eye technique before being restored to my mother in 1920, in a red and white hospital suit, a man whose true wounds were internal, his memories of the war to be arrayed in countless tales about *his* war.

She got him back, frail and embattled, but still only nineteen and handsome, with thick black hair still (although his own mother had to wait a full year before the war office discovered he was alive). They were married much later. Enter his lad, at ten years of age, who accompanied him on the nightly excursion to the cenotaph to share with the few other survivors (Stephen Race, Bill Woodcock) the feeling of "having got through" as D.H. Lawrence said of them.

To grow up among war heroes was somehow embarrassing. I remembered the way conversation ground to a halt when he entered for his libation at the Duke of York pub, as if the crowd awaited a speech or a mental breakdown. Then conversation resumed, he not having spoken, awed by the nightly event. This grew into an almost daily tale from the trenches, and his fund of memories swelled and got bolder. Mother had banned the very topic of war, so we waited to start until the first notes of her piano sounded as her teaching stints began.

That was how I became, for a while, an expert on the war, in my improvised and unmilitary way, becoming a veritable tripehound during 1939-45. War, into which Neville Chamberlain had plunged us, became the *sine qua non* of the breakfast table, smothered in oats, bran, and fried egg. Around seventeen, I replaced my father with literature, saw much less of him than before, but still remembered the bloody memories I had formed at his nimble, erudite hands.

My father, you see, was a dead man, restored to life, and I besieged him with questions about the afterlife, on which he drew a perfect blank. He remembered coming round after the shell had gone off, and being surrounded with Blood's body, but nothing else. I filled in for him, anxious to investigate the unknown (as always), loading my head with sanguinary dreams, the barking of gruff corporals, and the shrieking of his mother on hearing the false report of his death.

My point, lugubrious as it may sound, was to get my father in his grave, at 75, not a bad innings for someone reported long ago as dead. Once he was gone, he qualified for my bizarre category of UFO. Like them, he had not much to say, and said it well, opening up the whole vista of the unsaid, except that being the emphatic but sparing speaker that he was, bits of his actual dialogue sprang to guide me through life, to this very day: "You could trust a German, unlike the French"; "You have all my good wishes, my lad"; "There I was on the coast of France with the German army to face"; and hundreds more, each couched in his unique brand of subliterary military language, the high points of his three-and-a-half years in the trenches.

As I say, with my father dead, his incinerated corpse washed over into the world of the UFOs. But, I reasoned, was he silent enough to join forces with them, the masters of keeping mum? I decided yes, allying his *obiter dicta* with their unsaid volumes, somehow linking his standard utterances to their habitual silence. You see how I smuggled him in through the back door, pronouncing the same formulas time and again until I heard them from a great distance away, saying *there he goes again, I've heard it all before*. In this way, his spoken language became unspoken, no longer heard, and this reminded me of the UFOs (whose silence was as blank as his).

Armed with twin silences, I did my best, taking my father for granted and taking the UFOs in the same spirit, filling my mind with all they *could* have said. The problem was my father's easy amiability. You almost always knew what he was going to say, whereas they were silent from the word go. I imagined them born without tongues, a glitch on God's part, or recoiling from human atrocity, speaking in tongues to people who could hear them. No good. It still made no sense. Not a single one of all the human contacts they had made reported convincing speech.

The Travis Waltons by the thousands failed the language test, reporting only the merest fragments of Alien speech, as likely as not the result of talking to oneself.

Who cared anyway? Thousands, apparently, dying to know what the Aliens said, but fobbed off with sterile accounts of what they did with their human captives, reaming them out, emasculating more than a few, practicing skull and brain science with impetuous disregard. Always provoking pain and disgust, stealing half-formed children, and newly crippled adults. But what was said? Only the meagerest hints of their backchat, from thousands of reported encounters.

Surely the Aliens could hardly contain themselves as they discovered unprecedented features of human anatomy, calling out to one another, "Come and see this one, he has a deviated rib cage" or "Would you believe it, this one's balls are transparent." Or, even extremer, "Behold: the first symptom of cloppydoggerel intercourse, otherwise known as Algerian swont." Hundreds of these as they probed and tickled, heedless of the pain they caused, besotted with the new. I could hardly contain myself just thinking about them all.

Snapped out of it by a battered package of mail (months late thanks to slow delivery), I learned about the death of an old friend (breast cancer), someone I thought of as a lissome, witty young woman, a poet and literary critic with a talent for ferreting out fresh talent for the magazine she edited. Dead at a young age, cut off in her prime. It didn't bear thinking about.

I, much older than she, persisted in my obtuse way, much bemused by the memory of my mother, who soldiered on until 94, when she succumbed to a broken thigh, result of a surprise guest who burst in upon her when dozing. Her last words, "I have begun to die," evoked her continuous nobility in the teeth of destruction, willing to die but not altogether impressed by the beginnings of it. They all go under the hill, as Aubrey Beardsley said, some preceding others.

I rehearsed my long list of the dead and gone, easily twelve, some of them in their midtwenties, querying the point of it all. Born in order to die? In Outer Mongolia or wherever else? Snapped out of living for what? To be reborn as a rat or raccoon, according to your cosmology.

This, trapped again in my resentful way, brought me back to earth, to the Aliens, puzzling as ever, debating whether their live forms had anything in common with the dead of our planet, secreted underground in the millions. *Cui bono*—what's the use? Leaving behind them a sheaf of leaves or a pile of books. The living dead of the UFOs seemed more alive than our recent dead, or our distant ones. Full of promise, awaiting only the supreme signal to twitch into life again. Was I fooling myself? Fending off the supposition that life doesn't amount to more than this— impotently signaling since the Dark Ages to no purpose? A multitude of question marks adorned my script when I grew philosophical. *They do not like us, they are waiting for us to grow up,* I thought. *They are waiting for the first clean planet, in which no one has died.* Ridiculous.

They were waiting for an absence of violence, then? Some hope. They were waiting for instruction on how to proceed, because the guidebook had been left at home by some improvident jerk, light-years away? Surely they could send an envoy to retrieve it. Surely one had left already, was pounding the ether to get home fast, before the time permit expired. Maybe even a relay team, composed of sleepers who successively came to life, pacing one another into the jaws of oblivion until the last one reached home, only to find his home planet a cinder on touchdown. There would be a cold planet to greet him, a paltry breakfast for a great man whose helter skelter trip around the universe came to naught.

Rather than repeating experiments in nullity, I let my mind flow with possibility, at least to the extent of telling myself that the Aliens were silent, as my parents now were silent. No one was aboard, which gave me the lovely opportunity of saying that the superstructure was there all right, and the requisite instruments of flight, but *hollow*. The Aliens, rather than bother themselves with repeated sallies at the human condition (which they found repulsive and monotonous) had elected to do it all by remote control, what we would call fly-by-wire.

In this way, they could intercept from all over the cosmos the same stupefying message time and again that read "Not ready" or, in the local Mongolian argot, *yaduu* (poor). This enabled them to devote time, of which they had an infinite supply, to more responsive but still unsatisfactory projects elsewhere in the cosmos. Maybe Earth ranked low on the list of unworthy projects, maybe our violence was chickenfeed compared to that of many others.

The nefarious nature of this escape clause impressed more than it should have. I rolled the words around in my mouth—*empty, hollow*—until I tired of the motion. This was a breakthrough, and I rejoiced in the find, able at last to concentrate on other things, language and food, for instance, without racking my mind on a cosmic puzzle. For it was very different to say that they were *silent for un-*

known reasons than to say the UFOs were *empty*.

I was tempted to leave it at that, except that having come so far I wished to go further, expecting to find something even beyond emptiness. Perhaps I had discovered the Eldorado of space travel, the way one was booted up the line from null—*empty*—to something else, something more enticing than a human form.

For the present, I remained satisfied. Why should they waste time on a civilization not yet out of the Stone Age? Keep in touch with it, but no more than that? Maybe Earth itself was the winner of a very bad lot, yet one day would at last merit their full attention.

It was just a matter of waiting it out, never losing hope in face of the millions slaughtered by Hitler, Stalin, the Japanese, Pol Pot, and the rest. Maybe millions of years. But the UFOs would wait, I reassured myself, gleaning a little more hope.

FOUR

Once liberated from the need to imagine eavesdroppers scattered among the windows of the UFOs, gaping in wonderment at our earthly cavalcade, I breathed a sigh of comprehensive relief and saw things normally. No one at the window. There never had been. I harked back to all the conversations with UFO zealots I had read, and not one had mentioned an Alien face at the window, looking about in amazement, boredom, or sympathy as we went about our daily tasks.

How refreshing to find no one at home, no one appointed watchdog over us, the whole surveillance done with camera-like machines, images fed back to base at the space of light. All our doings for the Alien viewers, lolling in their chairs at whatever angle, discussing human behavior amply, and good-humoredly condemning us as too brutal. In the end, it felt wholesome to be thus invigilated by sky-wizards, or whatever, that clicked and clacked among the teleological finery aboard the spaceship of the moment.

I could well see how they would film us for hours, and then move on to richer pastures, not revisiting for as long as an Earth-month or an Earth-year. Thousands of spaceships could do that, varying their speed and then zooming off again. I imagined how much of our *caravanserai* they missed when all the movies were logged. A kiss here and there, a divorce threatened, a war declared, a finding that birds have no vocal apparatus, a shade of duck egg blue missed. I missed things too, as we all miss something or other in the pageant of our daily lives.

Too bad, but I would guess that the record of human antics stored aboard the UFOs exceeded that of the homegrown variety by a factor of millions. Surely it was not like them to do things by halves, not when the speed of light was commonplace and black holes *de rigueur*. How exciting to exist in their voyeur's purview. At times forgotten, no doubt, but an earth encapsulated by an Alien memory devoted to instant recall.

Musing thus, I remembered (how to forget?) my own UFO, that poolside interlude in June, so long ago. And nothing since. It put my mind to the test, hovering there a good twenty minutes: huge, buff-colored, and (when it arrived and departed) lightning fast. To think that such a thing was *empty* (apart from technical apparatus) was wild, but it stirred my daydreams. The vision of the remote control necessary widened my sense of space prodigies. *Imagine that*, I said to myself, *I was as an infant until now.*

Gradually I expanded my scope to include things I had heard about without witnessing, such as these shapes:

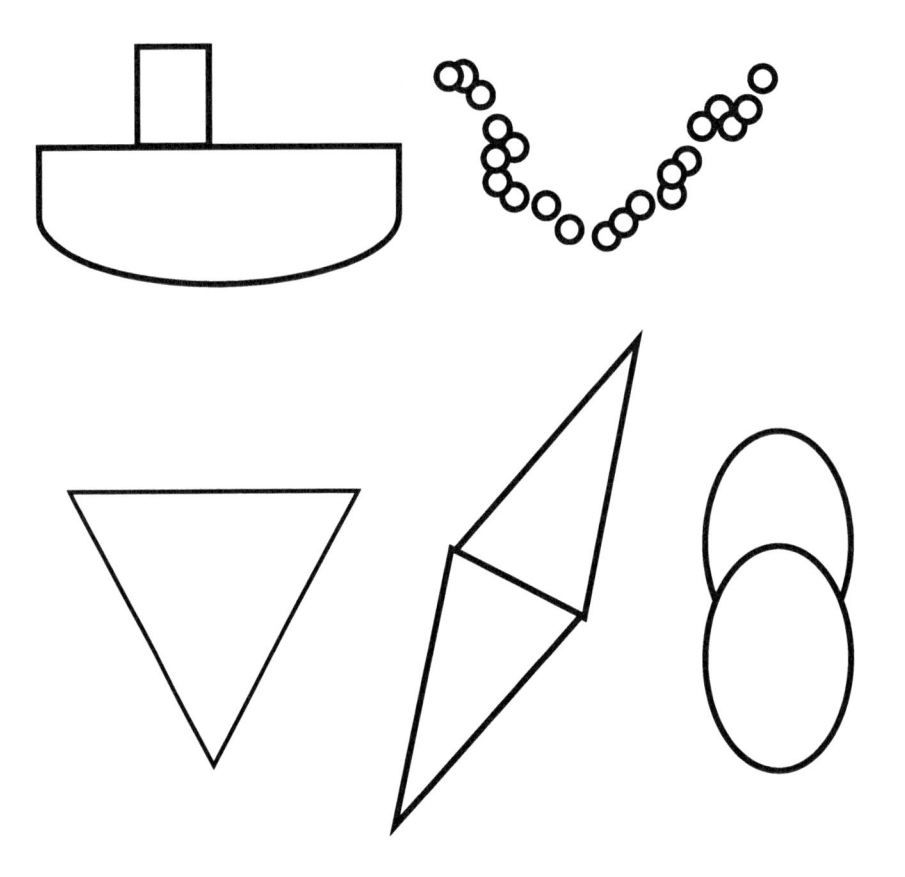

Many spoke of such things, sometimes not actually seen, but imagined, plausible constructs for an active mind, waiting for the right day for revelation. I imagined, transposing planes into UFOs, in ascending order from Ercoupes, Cessnas, Mooneys, into the realm of jets, which of course were a rough approximation of the real thing. It was delicious to think of the UFOs traveling at the speed of light, far beyond the capabilities of military aviation of our day. Stealth disembodied, minus pilot or pilots. Plainly, the UFOs, so far, had no warlike intentions upon us, and who knew when they began their scrutiny of the human species. The Stone Age? Maybe. Long before Leonardo da Vinci, perhaps in the kingdom of the dinosaurs, as earthbound creatures marveled at what was popping over their heads without ever landing.

I knew of one person, Philip Corso, who had actually seen his first Alien, rigged in a tomb-like suit with outsized head and four-fingered hands, about five feet tall. Dead, of course. The military guard who had directed Corso to this exhibit confessed he had been unable to get his head straight ever since, but that was some vagary of his own. Corso had seen, noted, and proceeded on his merry way. The interesting thing was the Alien had not uttered a solitary sound to anybody before it died.

Peering out at the dwindling Mongolian day, I noticed in the distance a bizarre procession of crates and bodies negotiating the walk to our dingy quarters with difficulty. It was not that much of a haul, but they were making heavy weather of it, burdened by what seemed to be ski poles, heaps of comfortless bedding, boxes of various shapes, musical instruments, parcels some of which kept flying off, some retrieved, some not, and at the rear end of this untidy parade, a gigantic figure, perhaps a golem or a menhir, bringing up the rear with jerky staggers, clearly a walk of some kind, Elephant Man or Dracula, doing his best to keep up, but falling behind at regular intervals with falsetto cries of dismay. Perhaps he would have been better off leading the *cortège* as they fumbled their way up the incline, shedding their load as they staggered towards—what? Surely not me, the only odd duck in their midst, marooned in constant mind fugues about a race of beings whose masterstroke was that they were not there.

I turned away from the window to concentrate on a glass of beer, but glanced up some moments later to see the entourage a couple of yards farther back, pulled by the last man.

Caught up in the sight of two steps forward, three steps back, I chose a piece of gum to chew and settled in for an afternoon's viewing, intoxicated by the view of someone attempting the impossible. I had heard of snow climbers trying in vain to regain their feet, but always failing until their impetus gave out and they accepted their new and last role as a prisoner of the crevasse.

I had no idea of what I was gaping at, electric train or prisoner-of-war morass. Some sort of train it would have to be, with my defective vision sweeping them all into one elongated box. Half an hour later, thanks to the initiative of some of the bearers who shed parcels and other impediments, they had progressed upward several yards. I divined they were heading right for me, God knows why. I was ensconced in my eyrie on a makeshift plateau (a small bump in the ground). By whose authority? A bolder man than I would have swept out and interrogated them fast. But I surrendered to the hypothesis of the event, waiting for the first knock on the door announcing the failure of their mission and asking what to do now.

No knock came, and I roused myself to see what was going on. The conga line, now divided into three groups, all shedding their loads, lined up at my door. They were waiting for the last man to catch up with them, which he did with an extraordinary amount of puffing, his non-face shrouded behind a white mask, his torso adapted to an antique wheelchair, the whole apparition masked with whatever parcels and highly reinforced boxes of plunder or provisions.

Still no knock, but I sensed someone in their party was steeling himself to do it. Still no knock, and I realized they were at the wrong house, at least until the knock came, a slow motion, faint and interrupted thing, and I opened up. Chunk-chunk went the mess of contents in the April breeze.

"Who's there?" No answer.

The figure in the wheelchair blurted through his mask: "Don't know me? It's *me*," he mumbled, finally doffing his protective armor to reveal a face soaked in sweat and gore, and at last I recognized his now high-pitched voice. Beehive hair. It was my old friend Lomax, the worse for wear, his legs swathed with bandages and breathing hard.

"It's me, come all the way to see you."

I marveled at the preposterousness of it all, lost for words. He repeated what he had said, in a voice even higher.

"I can see that," I said in a broken, genuinely affected voice. "How's the leg, the legs?"

"Next year, maybe. They don't break easily, and when they do, all hell breaks loose." "The snows of Ithaca," I murmured, for once giving way to nostalgia. "Pike's Peak," I suggested.

"No, it was *Greek* Peak."

"Dangerous," I said to him, knowing those snowy forests well.

"Not if you're careful. I wasn't."

"Too bad. And now you've come here to rest up."

"I came because you needed me. I knew the way."

I did indeed know he knew, but I wondered about his conspicuous generosity. Coming all that way for me, just because I sounded down or maybe delusional. Had he flown in with those legs? Surely he had not walked?

"Flew," he said. "Then the National Railroad all the way to Zamchid Station."

I inspected his legs even as he feebly gesticulated at the door. Then I belatedly invited him in, struck dumb by the enormous range of his purchases: small boxes, big boxes, a whole assembly of climbing boots, sturdy boxes of pills which betokened a long stay (easily top-ping his previous sojourn with me), and a bizarre assortment of tennis rackets, cricket bats (!), soccer balls (not one of them used) exposing pigskin hides of vertiginous pink. Was he going to start organizing a team, or teams, handicapped as he was?

"The bearers," he said abruptly, sculling around in the doorway. "They haven't been paid." I fumbled the right amount, scarcely knowing what I was doing, handing out approximate quantities of *nogoon,* shirking the more official *togrog,* which I had trouble even saying. Finally they went away once it was clear their extortion had come to a profitable end. My traveling companion had returned, at great expense of life and limb, and I was in his debt a thousand-fold. But, I asked myself, did I now need him or his help with the UFOs? Had he new suggestions to toss into the pot, based on experience greater than mine—although he was not a believer?

In no time, we were taking tea together, deferring until later our problem of sleeping arrangements. Somehow his legs seemed even longer this time around, which I attributed to the wrapping that festooned them. What was clear was that his clothes were muddy beyond belief, and he had made a gigantic effort to be with me in what he assumed was my hour of need. Hail the conquering hero. Achilles on Viagra could not have done more.

The Invisible Riviera

"How goes the eternal problem?" he asked when the ritual observances had been satisfied.

"The problem of what?"

"I mean your old friends the UFOs. Have you come to any decision?"

I told him, but I could see that the recital of their invisibility tired and provoked him. He asked if I could consider making an end of it and devote my time to the local language, say, or to the myths that surrounded us. Genghis Khan, for instance, the lord of lords.

"Yes," he added, "he has eighteen million descendants living nowadays. How's *that* for panspermia?"

"Fabulous," I answered.

"Indeed, he wasn't only fearsome to look at, he dominated the line of men living in this region of the former Mongol empire who carry the same Y-chromosome. If you choose to look at it that way."

"Thirteenth century?"

"Thirteenth indeed."

For some reason, his allusion to the thirteenth century disturbed me. Perhaps making me feel my age. It was a poor response to his broken legs, but I felt he was somehow enjoying them. Constantly shifting them, one leg followed by the next, he seemed a bleached automaton, surely larger than when he went away. The room was full again, both of his aroma and his super-presence. *I must wash his linen for him*, I thought. Had he come all this way for *that*? I offered my services, as blandly as I could, like an offering to Genghis Khan. He demurred, saying in his distracted way, "Later, after I've had my sleep."

He had come to stay, all right, and I felt a tide of resentment bubble up. He had journeyed all this way merely to be nursed, when I had the problem of the UFOs to deal with: not exactly a piece of cake. As it was, the tiny receptacle of my room was now filled to overflowing with his impedimenta, spilling off the bed at certain points, tumbling on the floor. When he made not the slightest motion to unpack to make the burden of his presence smaller, I bit my tongue and told myself there would be time for all that later when palaver of Genghis Khan versus the UFOs would be in full flower. *Careful with him,* I instructed myself, *he's one of the walking wounded, apt to work himself to death.* You don't look a gift Lomax in the mouth. I propped him up, relegated the wheelchair to a lofty perch out of the way, and fussed with wounds, eventually washing him down in the most Christian way available to me, murmuring quietly as he went to sleep entangled in a horsehair blanket. I unrobed his feet, finding them beyond me (too much badly bloodstained plaster of Paris), and left him to sleep off the miles.

Outside, a gaggle of locals still hung on, discussing his arrival, his bloodstained legs, and his endless supply of boxes. I had forgotten to ask after his two Ithaca neighbors, and what they felt about his trekking such a distance with impeded feet. Surely they had dissuaded him over the nightly spaghetti.

When he had recovered the better part of his good nature, which had been cramped by sleeplessness and frost, he opened up one of the multitudinous packages that had accompanied him on his plane and railroad trek to Ulan Bator. This was a trapezoid rectangle, enclosed in tissue and brown paper. I peered hard as he unwrapped it by the kerosene stove, guessing what it might hold. A model train, with severed coaches? A Virgin Mary to pray to in the long hours of sleeplessness? A chunk of hematite rock destined for polishing and eventual presentation to the Mongolian Artist's Exhibition Hall in Ulan Bator? Or a miniature traditional Mongolian *deel*, a long loose gown cut in one piece with a high collar?

I eyed the monster as it shed its wrappings, surely arranged to have me believe it was indeed a model train, Virgin Mary, a piece of local rock, a *deel*. As one gave rise to another I lost heart and started again. The carton demanded multiple unwrappings, giving me chance to cancel speculation several times before the object revealed itself at last. I even suspected him of having wrapped mere wrapping as a hoax, actually making me think that all this parcel post was purely for effect and amounted to nothing.

Finally, the mysterious object appeared: a model plane with what seemed like an electric motor, a cute toy of a thing, but worth his hauling all the way to Ulan Bator? Green and white, the plane measured eight inches or so, a high wing with a conventional tail and a standard-looking undercarriage. Not bad, as planes went, but no cigar. I yearned for the planes I had flown in my youth, giants with four-foot wingspans and capable of bypassing you with a whoosh as they took flight.

"This one is special," he said, belying its tame structure. "Demo later on, when my mood has settled down and my legs have eased."

I wondered at all this drama, readying myself for an anti-climax whenever it took flight. If ever. His most recent trophy was a letdown. Somehow I would have settled for the Virgin Mary or the *deel*, but here he was, two broken legs, and a heap of no doubt similar presents lugged all the way to Ulan Bator for no purpose (I presumed) than to disappoint me with a camel's droppings. I bit my tongue, admired the plane, and disappeared into a book, a piece of froth by one Leila Hadley, but enough to calm my soul. He, in his way, caught up on sleep, and I began to pray that he would leave the rest of his parcels unopened.

The next thing I remember was his presence outside, bullying the locals in spite of his crippled legs. He had, I don't know how, fished his wheelchair down and arranged himself inside it. He was not going to be bed-bound if he could help it. A man in his predicament was entitled to bully the local gentry. They had come merely to look at him, nothing else. And he had responded, in English (I surmised), given them a handful of assorted cash and sent them packing, leaving them to figure out the rate of exchange. I tried to explain to him the art of *nogoon*, but he cast me aside with the *sobriquet* of "blasted foreigner" and left me to get on with Leila Hadley and her sea stories of burly yachtsmen.

To change subjects fast, in case he overwhelmed me one day with *nogoon*, and tiring of Leila Hadley's exploits as "Hadley" (which the crew dubbed her), I let my mind wander again in the realms of the UFOs. They had their uses after all.

When descending to our level the Aliens made the best of things, I reckoned, lip-reading or using some other device peculiar to them. It sounded plausible and maybe it was, but something unsatisfactory about the whole enterprise invaded my thoughts and wouldn't let go.

Was I sentimentalizing them? Half-deciding to let it go at that and abandon them to the unheard predicates and spiritual ditties of no tone, I rebelled again. So I resuscitated them, broadening my scope, imagining for them a whole new range of silent champions with which they could amuse themselves while waiting for the heyday of the human brute to end and the Golden Age to begin. A long wait, if you asked me. Indeed it could never happen, humanity being extirpated by an irresistible comet in 2012, say, the favorite scenario of most astronomers.

I contented myself with designing new shapes for the silent Aliens, deserting my old notion of automata aboard the space ships. Playing all manner of autotelic games, and (on occasion) doubling and tripling up to play all manner of sports with one another while waiting. In this way, I enriched my supply of Aliens, and allowed them a modicum of yells and disappointed mutters as a comedy of errors unfolded in their spaceships. This was much better than before. I still could not understand their yells and whimpers, an odd mixture of pleonastic blurts and half-cries, but I didn't even try to.

Sometimes my brain betrayed me, distending things, or making them smaller, sometimes pushing objects out of sight, at other times shrinking them down to invisibility. Was it my eyes misrepresenting me, thanks to some fluke in the pupil? It didn't matter. I had other things wrong with me as well from strokes to erysipelas, from migraine to St. Vitus's dance.

I wished for sane goings-on, but received something else, some vagary of the internal body. Sooner or later, everyone's body goes wrong, and you start making mistakes until the end, but it remains up to you to take it as best you can. In my case, at least I'd suffered no more than one malady at a time.

In Light Lomax's case, his two legs were trial enough, but there was more, occupying him with trips to China and Vietnam, where he purchased exotic cures, as well as resplendent suits of purple silk, and flew homeward again to his little flat, and his raised steel-sprung mattress high up in the rafters, he being averse to ground level beds. On the other hand, he seemed to have survived Chernobyl, thus far at least, and was a geek loaded with money.

He was equipped with a goodly dose of pelf, which belied his passion for sleeping in railroad tunnels, Chernobyls, and unsatisfactory lean-tos while away on foreign expeditions, which he countered by indulging in expensive and liberally capacious suits (he was a tall man, as I have said). A creature of contrasts, self-educated to a profound degree, he brought up his twelve-year-old son in the same fashion, parking him with friends during his long trips abroad.

I would not have been surprised if he launched one day into the crabbed local language, *logrog* and *nogoon,* handling it with dexterity for a non-linguistic man who just happened to be a master of all sorts of lingo, including Khalkh Mongol. He had been here before I met him, undoubtedly, and mastered the local slang before I even knew of its existence.

Impeded as he was, he cut a striking figure in the wheelchair (he was big as I say), and imposing with his showers of parcels, which he rarely inclined to open, not for supplementary air supplies, emergency wheelchairs, or tributes of lavishly dressed silk, each from somewhere more exotic than the last. As for Aliens, he did not take them seriously, tolerating them perhaps because he had a devout fan aboard, but one with specialized taste, not given to all the gossip pertaining to UFOs. Whether he found me less of a fanatic or more, I scarcely knew, but I was aware of the general current of his disapproval, his relegation of such matters to the category of not worth getting excited over or sending to hell for duplicates.

He bore with me for old time's sake, having seen me through college, where we were roommates, a couple of ill-starred romances, two transient ischemic strokes, and a teaching job. From the last, a strongly suggested leave of absence, just because I had changed my field of interest from Elizabethan Literature to Exobiology. Fair enough. I had become a stranger to myself. But not to Light, it seemed. He remained steadfast and resilient. For my part, I'd seen him through a parcel of life that would have scotched lesser men, including the death of his wife, leaving him with a son to raise on his own.

More I could not say of him. The crippled version of himself was a stranger to me, as well as numerous attributes only recently arrived at (his pretended ignorance of the local *patois*, for instance), or his silence regarding his son and his two roommates back in the snowy gardens of Ithaca.

I guessed it was a problem of getting to know people halfway. They were always outstripping you with portions of their being brought into play at the last moment, as they began the dreadful tumult of aging, then the ultimate surrender to that or this disease, in pain or in somnolence, each in his own way longing for the end to begin.

After a while he grew restless, which I took to be the infernal itch of his wounds. But I could be wrong. Maybe he was feeling genuinely better and wanted a daily regimen of activity. Whatever. He took to parading in the wheelchair, escorted by two or three out-of-work locals whom he plied with money. Where did he keep it all? Buried in the wrappings around his legs? I never found out the source of his supply, except that I was not invited to go along on the *caravanseri* of red bandages and extravagant talk.

The more I thought about him, the more I realized how little I knew the real Lomax. Not the blood soaked, bandaged Lomax, but the gregarious side, affable or convivial verging on treacherous. A man so big, you have to make allowance for his evil side, of which he, as befits, had more than his fair share. I had heard of little duplicitous men (I was one myself perhaps), but they never approached him in trickery. The fact that big men could be virtuous through and through did not occur to me. If there was spare footage, then some of it must be bad. Such my philosophy, earned in the hard school of experience.

By that token, it seemed obvious that his leg injuries were illusory, coined to impress the majority, as was his apparent good fellowship in flying out to Mongolia to see me through my hour of need. After all, no matter how many UFOs he'd seen, he was essentially a nonbeliever, doomed never to change his spots. As if his blood soaked legs and his pro-UFO sentiments were masks to be doffed whenever the true occasion arose.

This doubleness of his nature should have alerted me to something similar in myself, but no, human nature isn't built like that. Some are self-conscious, some not. He was brilliant, as many conceded. But capable of going too far, taking a yard when he deserved an inch. I was only latterly beginning to recognize that fact, too little and too late. Reforming zeal in people with white hair is not a popular folkway.

The Invisible Riviera

I kept my obsessions narrow. Silence or nothing. Why must all the millions of galaxies produce not a single voice serenading us? What is wrong? Could it be that the Aliens were searching for a comfortable new place to settle, and found Earth a poor and lonely job? Surely, the human search for a companionable planet would go on and on into the 2050s, unanswered, until at the last a weary UFO broke silence with: *We've looked everywhere in vain. You are the only possibility, and we spurn you. Just letting you know the truth.* That kind of exchange, bad-mouthing us, as we might have expected. The wars between the nations would go on.

Pardon the break in my voice. Such things are hard to say, evoking the image of chronic, permanent defeat, something awry in human nature, not enough Vitamin C, not enough aluminum. Which makes the human enterprise, wondrously wrought in several ways, a botch, until the year, say, 5000. I pitied the unsatisfied landless residents of the UFOs, looking and looking, taking a never-ending vow of silence. They had their standards, we ours. If they would not speak to us, we could hardly speak to them.

FIVE

I suspected him of turning his back on his latter-day eccentricity, insofar as he was in control of it at all. He used to be wilder, not actually subscribing to Alien visitors, but judiciously intimating chosen bits of UFO talk into everyday conversation, prating of boundary layers and event horizons, the discoveries of Nicolas Tesla and Harry S. Truman "are not constructed of any power on earth."

This gave the impression of one well-versed in his subject of extraterrestrial lore. He was trying to pass muster as one of the boys, and if truth be known, his philosophy was grounded in deep cynicism, like his having "seen" four examples of UFO flight, apparently without relish, delight, or holy discovery. He discussed them as if they were fried eggs, sunny side up, and left it at that, reserving a tiny bit of mystique for the off chance of the myth being true. For him, never Margaret Mead's candid explanation of "quiet, harmlessly cruising objects that time and again approach the earth."

She knew whereof she spoke, one of "us" from way back, giving the lie to Light Lomax and his skeptical cynical crew. Notice the emphasis she places on *harmless*, *quiet* objects. As if she knew no harm would come to us, despite whatever our local nationalities had in store. Perhaps only someone reared in the Southern Seas could be that generous with extraterrestrials.

Light Lomax, however, actually preferred war and all that went with it, not being of a warlike nature but extending the range of his *bonhomie* that far, letting war happen now and then for the passing good it did. I remembered my father's "war brings people together" and "war obliges people to cooperate." Such stilted speech came naturally out of people who had known nothing but war, as my father had, and it conferred no right to tamper with the tide. The earth had its good days now and then, not many it must be admitted, but a few here and there.

So it was Lomax's ambivalence that brought about the main rift in our dialogue, not something as touchy as Romanticism versus Classicism, or Big-Endians versus Little-Endians (with homage to Dean Swift), though such things had occupied us earlier. It was something of faith that occupied us now, agnostic faith maybe, but, when you came right down to it, a faith hacked and blunt. Take it or leave it. No wonder we quarreled in the shamefaced manner of the time, he the autodidact, me, the university man, both intent on winning the unfindable prize.

If only we could have left it at that, agreeing to differ and then forgetting the dispute forever. The issue had its tentacles deeply around us. It recurred in the most inconsequential conventional conversations, say about the merits of local butter (*tsötsgiin tos*) versus imported butter (*maasal*). It was a wasted conversation, threatening a conversion which did not take place. And it turned out that I found *tsötsgiin* impossible to say, never reaching the *tos*, so we ended our days on imported butter, glad to evade the claws of such a brutal language.

One of the things I noticed was that Lomax's supply of boxes was eroding perceptibly as he gave gifts to his hirelings. The more he gave, the more they turned up for booty, which included (as I peeked from my window) tin whistles, bazookas, effigies of Genghis Khan made in plaster-of-Paris, ancient-looking plastic fountain pens and sets of cheap tinted sunglasses. These they donned or otherwise arranged around their persons with glee while he watched the performance with evident relish, realizing (my assumption) that he had come home among his real people at last.

At times he half-rose from his chair, with an unsimulated flinch which bespoke genuine discomfort, lurching against the bandages with a fatidic air. Perhaps the whole business of the bandages was a spoof intended for public consumption. One day soon (maybe) he would arise in full glory, a man redeemed by tin whistles and imitations of Genghis Khan.

I hoped not, preferring my friend genuine even if irritating. But bound he stayed, always sinking back in his wheelchair with the motion of a soul reprieved. He had given his all, journeying to succor his friend in need. Such the myth of him as he surrounded himself with elementary caregivers awaiting the next gift. What would happen, I wondered, when the supply gave out and he was restricted to giving out grimy bandages instead? A fall in Light Lomax stock? A revelation of two bandaged legs well-healed?

In a word, I doubted him for the first time, setting aside the saga of the bandaged legs, the skepticism concerning UFOs. He was a mountebank through and through and not to be trusted in matters orthopedic. Once decided upon, the image stuck of his being a totally engrossing fraud, no longer the friend in need but an imposter of influence and gift giving. And it is not without a certain regret that I thus signaled the loss in his status as he, just a yard or two initially, shied away from me, eventually disappearing from sight along Zaluud Zaluuchuud Avenue past the General Post Office and Enkh Tayvan to Natsogdori Street, at which point I lost him among the concatenations of unpronounceable streets, he purposely (I thought) having selected the hardest-to-say as the route of choice, thus being obliged to make many romantic detours, distributing presents as he walked, winning friends galore as he half rose from his bandages, creaking and groaning, to present the latest gift.

Sooner or later he would arrive at the Sukhtaar Bulgan road to the southwest and the Nature Reserve, and then he would be lost for good, finally being emancipated from his wheelchair and freed for the open road back to—Ithaca? I envied his talent for making friends, even of a temporary nature, but I was my own introverted self (not given to fastidious friendships or long walks in enemy territory). I wished he had settled into one of the monasteries on his way, or would leave on one of the neighbor airports from which the yellow jetplane logo invited him to fly.

I noticed, as day succeeded day, how his moments became increasingly erratic. He stayed away longer, returning only in the early evening (I repeatedly found myself eating dinner alone, usually beef and Jodhpur lentils), with always an increasing commotion of arrival, as if he deplored having been away so long. Only a few days later he was out all night, tupping the local doxies from his wheelchair, hoisting skirts like a maniac in a hell of a hurry. I, who slept through these events, retained little of them apart from the several times when he awoke me with mumbled apologies and somehow got himself into bed, which reinforced my assumption about his wheelchair act being bogus. Somehow getting to sleep again, I craved the circumstances of old—when we did things together, shared similar thoughts, patronized the same doxies.

Things were different now, as I contemplated the stack of gifts to be given away to his cronies, who ministered to his every need with greed in their eyes and made obscene jokes about him behind his back.

It was no use protesting the comparative peace of our previous existence. He was a different man these days, fizzier and more abstruse, and what had been lively conversations had dwindled into stale, familiar ones. Many were the times we would arrive at the same conclusion in pretty much kindred syllables. I took this consanguinity (or whatever it was) as a mark of true kinship, rejoicing in the monotony of our near-agreement rather than in the obviousness of thinking alike. All that was gone. Our self-interruptions bore no resemblance to each other and faded away, fast as thought itself, a constantly diverging pattern of exclamations and babbles.

"I say," I would begin, "their word for goat is *yam*—."

"Like hell it is," he would say in response.

"Or heaven."

"You think."

"Honest."

"My fairy godmother's left teat."

This kind of exchange, or shuffling of rival views got close to monkey chatter, only making less sense. The word for it was *riposte,* or (an old word rescued from my word-hoard) *flyting,* but the essence of it was non-cooperation, the only technique remaining was to spite the other. Which we did quite readily, I lamenting the way friendship had declined into squabble.

Oh well, everything must have an end, even spite. Begun well, ending in ashes. It makes no difference in the long run how a thing was said and to whom. Just the ticket to drive me back to the UFOs, a mystery worth cogitating, even after death, provided you entered on the right wavelength.

After a while, during which I extended my diet to carp and pike (having found out the words for them), I ventured even further, discovering the names of Lomax's main three adherents: *Nugas, Tarvag,* and *Bodon Gakhai* (which I dealt with in truncated form). The three wise men of his entourage: *Nugas*, a pimply faced youth, beardless and scrawny, with slight deformity of the right leg; *Tarvag,* he of the sprawling red beard and distinctive baritone voice (a good broadcaster in the making?); and *Bodon G.*, a slightly older version of someone's grandmother, teethless and doddery thanks to some wasting disease. All in all a motley crew of hangers-on, more attracted by gifts than by the prospect of amputation. All of them about thirty years old.

I later found out that all three were named after local fauna—*Nugas* (duck), *Tarvag* (marmot), and *Bodon G.* (wild boar). I waited for them to tear Lomax to bits, but all I discerned was the gift of a golf ball, a tennis racquet, and (for *Bodon G.*) a shuttlecock, which all squirreled away in their saturnine exteriors, even *Tarvag*, whose corpulence had deep pockets. I was being initiated into local lore along with the language (partly), capable of seeing *Nugas, Tarvag,* and *Bodon G.*, without being much impressed: three Mongolians out for an acquisitive stroll.

They treated him with what looked like awe, to the full extent of their rudimentary vocabulary, and Lomax expressed himself to the minimum expected of him. He did not, would not, speak their language after all. Meanwhile, the supply of toys went down, delivered daily to scapegrace hoards off Khasbaatar Street or the Central Bus Terminal.

Quite plainly, Lomax wanted something from them, not aesthetic nor geographical, but dare I say spiritual, no matter how rudimentary it was. Something quite the reverse of UFOs, something tangibly ornate, something they disregarded from familiarity. Something tribal and petty. To tell the truth, I had no idea what he wanted from them, except something perhaps related to gold balls, tennis racquet, shuttlecock, all such finery. I was certain nevertheless that it must be spiritual, in the widest sense.

Out of sight now with his team of ne'er-do-wells for some much to be desired excursion among the *hoi polloi*, he seemed larger than ever in his plump anorak and winter-verging-on-summer cap. He no longer figured among welcome guests, arriving just as I drifted off to sleep, departing before I woke, a homunculus of a formerly big man, a wordless golem of secret assignments, whose pretensions were all faked.

Had he gone over to the enemy, or did some delicate portion of him still cling to the conversations we used to have, bristling amid the sign language he used for his henchmen? Was he actually preparing a gang for the next Mongolian war, or proposing a trip to China, south of here? Where he went, I know not to this day, but I knew the goodies would one day give out and giftless, naked, he would stare at the three men, before they decided what to do with him.

In the midst of mulling over Light Lomax and the root of his eccentricity, I allowed my mind to wander around, pausing at this or that scene of wonderment. I wondered why I found myself, as the idiom has it, where I was, instead of ordering my favorite Eggbeater Omelet Plain and mashed potato smothered in gravy, at Toojays deli where I could gape my fill at the square courtyard formed from long-lasting privet squares surmounted by buff-colored minarets and patrolled by roaming, well-fed cats. Visions of this paradise came and went, this home of loaves baked by the women of the house. Ah, Toojays deli was not perfect, but it would serve many a thousand delicious breakfasts before lapsing into oblivion, torn down for a parking lot.

There, the cooked egg had a heavenly tinge of brown, the mashed potatoes tasted of mushrooms (in which they had been scalded), and the plates themselves were wide, capacious, and sturdy while the rye bread that came with the egg was crusty and fresh. Twelve dollars at last count, twenty-four (natch) for two.

The Eggbeater came steaming hot, as did the mashed potato, and only the bravest dared touch either during the first few minutes of its entrancing state. Extra gravy by the ladleful (50 cents extra) and for true gourmands the whole thing repeated half an hour later, it was so good. Why go away from such a place? Drawn thither by friends is how I recollect it. (In search of an exquisite Mongolian breakfast.)

Why then, I repeat, did I go away? Not just because of the wanderlust of Lomax. A desire to see how the other half lived? Or to track Genghis Khan to his ultimate score? Something of that. And what of boredom, the old hag snipping at our heels. Some of her? Conceivably, but it was, for my part, the fear of growing old before my time, of not challenging the brain cells with doing battle once again.

Look at Light Lomax now, betrayed into deserting his old friend for the company of *Nugas, Turvag,* and *Bodon G.,* a trio of shady hangers-on at best. Small wonder I was increasingly driven to Toojays, in memory at least, for a modicum of what used to please me mightily. I add the UFOs, bewildering as my pursuit of them was turning out to be, these silent emissaries, surely the mere recording device sponsored by headquarters.

Beyond that theory it felt impossible to proceed. What if UFO activity was mainly confined to submarine duties, which remained largely uninvestigated by us although things were picking up in the benthics? A snowflake takes three months to fall the full distance to the bottom of the mid-ocean trench. Now who but an Alien is capable of dealing with that marvel?

As I saw less and less of Lomax, thanks to his devotion to his crew, I began to imagine things about him which were not true, but had a miniscule point—such as his wearing fishermen's sweaters. One could tell from the weave (Morse code knit and purl) whose body it was, no matter how chewn up by fishes the remains were. Thank goodness for idiosyncratic knitting patterns that enabled you to find your way among the dead.

I knew by heart the distinctive patterns of his two sweaters, but the image of drowning fishermen emboldened me to vengeful caricature. Lomax was not where he should have been, succoring his lonely friend, and his absence was beginning to take its toll of camaraderie, witty exchange, and sheer company. I could follow him, I supposed, wherever his daily and nocturnal comings and goings transported him, but something kept me back. I wanted his secret to remain—for the time being at least—which was my way of saying that I, too, in the fatuous guise of friendship, was not ready to let go. Little of the old Light Lomax survived, but it might come back by dead of night with a jolly laugh and a swipe across my naked knees.

You see how it felt, too rapid a transition between full-blooded proximity and half-blooded disinterest. Too sudden for the likes of me, too fickle and tendentious.

Groping around for an image to assuage my condition, I hit on one from the coffee world, a circular strip of corrugated paper, helping you clutch your brimming, steaming cup of java like a friend. Coffee-less, I clutched, investing with all my might, anxious to close my eyes and find at last my former ally when I opened them, radiant with morning smile and saying, *How did you sleep, good friend?* Goodbye to all that.

Instead, I could see his image, sent along with hundreds of others to dig a trench thirty feet wide under Chernobyl itself, workmen in the heat toiling with bare backs and doffed masks, never told about what one minute's labor would do to their future. In the end, they filled in the trench with concrete, and transferred the team (all suffering radioactive burns) to an improvised hospital, there to let them suffer in agonized peace.

What had the swarthy (by flashlight) Chernobyl guards said to Lomax in Russian as he lay within the perimeter, huddled up in his skivvies? In that forbidden zone of hell, who knew how many *röntgens* it took? "Wake up, *tovarisch*. You are in the forbidden zone. I could shoot you for this. And all the better for you in the long run." Lomax had gathered himself up and crossed to the other side of the broken barrier, cursing, as was his habit, because he was just getting off to sleep.

All this Lomax had relayed to me, mute witness to a tale of horror, if I could believe it at all. What had he been doing within the radioactive zone? And what of the truculent guard? Had he too been exposed? How could he not? If so, he had been sentenced to a short life and could look forward to little, merely replaced when his time was up.

I marveled at how well Lomax had survived this interview with death. Perhaps, though I doubted it, he had been preserved for another fate, such as paralysis of both legs while awaiting the Almighty's final displeasure? I felt the old-new resentment taking over, the sense that whatever happened to him now was his own fault, be it radioactivity or the life of a cripple. The latter was the slower to act of the two, the former was the quicker, penetrating deep into the bone, eyes glazing, heart faltering.

How could I be such a poltroon to my recent friend? I hardly knew, but felt some acid animus for him, protesting one thing but seeking another. What would happen when the supply of toys gave out, as it soon would? Back home to Momma, all forgiven, with all the old hangers-on, *Nugas, Tarvag, Bodon G.*, passed to the rubbish dump? A likely fate. More likely they would be promoted to second-class retainers and dressed for the part with a private dog sled for company, stationed downriver at the International Tourist Camp in case of emergency.

My mind was running away with me, an old failing I could never manage to quell. Suddenly, an unorthodox thought would sprout wings and take off for God knew where, leaving me behind, the passive host. It was one way of escaping fickle friends and the unsayable problems of absent UFOs.

I realized I had had no thoughts of going back to Ithaca, land of gorgeous gorges and high taxes. I had set out to Mongolia with plans to return, which made me wonder what would happen when my supply of pills gave out, especially the Ritalin, on which I depended to keep me buoyant. Would a supply supply itself, or would I reach a down-at-heel terminus, begging any passing UFO to bow down and take me up into the bowels of the plane for further experimentation.

There I would no doubt fall prey to some arcane disease, an ossified hematoma of something or other, tabulated with stultifying efficiency by an Alien machine. I wished for more. In a sub-acute rush of frenzied longing, I longed for—what? So much, so many, that I could not keep count of them, but was aware of them without being able to identify one from another.

You see how easily I transposed my old friend into a being remote and aloof, just for changing his friends around somewhat. Anyone that sensitive deserved hanging, before he polluted the world with his intense ungratified desires. But you know, when you have reached the age of discernment, you lose control, you no longer wish things otherwise, but *so*. Just to have them so beats any opposition, as long as it is *exactly so*.

Were I younger, it would not matter as much, maybe not at all. But the faintest shade of difference makes a world of change, and one perhaps irreversible to boot. I am talking about minor changes, infinitesimal ones, which make vicious inroads on established codes of behavior.

"Goodbye, old friend," I said.

"Goodbye, cantankerous changeling."

"Goodbye, to you, and goodbye to *Nugas, Tarvag,* and *Bodon G.,* keepers of your faith whose supply of chocolates, balls of all kinds, and fireworks is bound to run out."

"Goodbye, nerd. Another must sustain you now."

"Rome wasn't built in a day," I said.

"Neither was Mongolia."

And that said, I at once began to track him, wherever he ended up, rubbing beards with Genghis Khan, or bloody bandages with the natives. I wondered what he did, which impulse drove him to excess.

I sidled outside, viewing far and near for a premature sign of him. But no. He had to be further away, although the Yurt-shaped Temple or the Dashchoylon Monastery would have given him a good place to skulk in, not to mention the German and North Korean consulate buildings. Down further the Romanians and Hungarians beckoned, but it could be any store, exhibition hall, or museum which held him and his blood-bolted secrets, his quizzical hangers-on. What if I found him, what should I say? "Still trying to learn the language, Lomax?" or "Still not tired of the team, Light?" It remained to be seen. Off I trotted in search of my old friend, regretting the absence of the four-wheel drive recommended by the Tourist Bureau, wondering how soon, if ever, I would reach the "flat" area of the steppe, where vehicles cut their own way through the wilderness.

It was time, I decided, to do something about his peripatetic ways, and the first step was to find him. The spectacle of a white-haired man in Western clothes seeking the whereabouts of a man in a wheelchair, in a foreign country where neither spoke the other's language, cried out for interpreters. It might have seemed easy, but it wasn't, describing the wheelchair. They didn't know what I had in mind, and at best thought me imitating a dragon or yeti.

I soon gave up, after flailing my arms about this way and that in a vain attempt at pantomime. I ended up seeking the guidance of the police, polite but ignorant of what I was after. I suppose it would have helped to equip myself with a phrase-book before leaving the house, but I was in too much of a hurry. Besides, what was the language for *wheelchair,* a word-puzzle to begin with? If Lomax kept his mouth shut, he probably appeared like any normal Mongol abroad for an outing. I tried the names—*Nugas, Tarvag, Bodon G.*—mispronouncing them (Nuga, Charv, Bodin), to no use: the populace stared at me, a man from Mars, whatever I mumbled, and at times I almost clapped my hand to my mouth in shame for how I mangled their craggy language.

After an hour of this, and unpronounceable street names, I located a bench and made an effort to regroup. And moments later Lomax appeared, large as life, minus his crew for once (the gifts finally beginning to give out).

"Out for a walk. Good for you," he said in hail-fellow well-met English.

"Looking high and low for you."

Lomax stumbled a little, then transferred himself to the bench. He looked weary and blasted from his outing.

"Out prospecting for a pick-up?" he said with false joviality.

"No," I said, "It is you I seek."

"For what?"

"Company."

"Oh that," he said. "Why?"

I fumbled an answer, something about foreign languages and the sound of a homely voice, even though I meant company in the real naked sense of a body to talk to. I left it at *company,* suspecting he wasn't up to buddy talk. He seemed stiff and gaunt, maybe going without food. I asked, having in mind Jodhpur lentils and beef, but he shied away, perhaps reluctant even to name it for fear of transgressing a local taboo.

"I've been sampling the local color."

"What color?" I said. "Which?"

"All colors," he said.

"The women."

"I haven't had a sexual thought," he said.

Liar. He should have remembered at least the supreme moments.

"I've been too busy."

"Doing what?"

"Coming to terms with two broken legs, if you remember."

"Oh, you are. Well, bully for you."

He had on his arrogant face. Stood up with difficulty, and lowered himself into the chair with conspicuous sighs. Instinctively, I leaned forward to help him, but he stopped me with one brush of a hand, installing himself rather nimbly, then wheeling away. I reviewed the chance that the wheelchair was a ruse and that he slipped out of it the instant I turned my back. Something suggested a shift in his behavior, but added up to nothing. He had gone where he had gone, and that was that. He had begun to disappear from me. Something was awry, but what?

Something that made him less of a man than he had been before. The plain fact that he was somehow cheating me, in spite of everything, hurt me. Why was he behaving so? What had gotten into him?

I ransacked my brain for what had provoked him to this, working into some lame conclusions. My brain was a dangerous neighborhood, I knew that for a start. Perhaps, beneath his wraps and wadding, he was wearing liquid handcuffs popped there by some zealous policeman intent on a new variation of restraint called violation of stranglehold. You see how my brain was working, using wilder and wilder speculations to fend off his insult? I even free-associated him with Hans von Ohain and Alexander Lippisch, two of my favorite airplane designers (though long since forgotten by the crowd). And with miscellaneous betrayals such as Coffin Corner (old RAF slang for dangerous place to fly through), Operation Drumbeat (a Nazi attack on New York), and such arbitrary seeming words as Astrid Bypass and *Colibri* (hummingbird). My brain yammered for Japanese Santa Clauses, American sagwaggies, and Nazi bombers otherwise known as the vermin of the skies.

No help. My room, chaste as usual, remained mute and peaceful. Whatever had become of Lomax remained the same. No hellions from downstairs entreated me, no one offered me food, the world stopped. Lomax was as silent as any UFO, and as blank, but surely valued because of that. I had long regarded English as the tosspot of all the random allusions language is open to, the infernal mother of all literary seasons, but this was one of those that escaped her: a word for the friend who never came back.

I realized that, down the road apiece, he might return, but that was not the same thing as the bald shock of lapse for unknown reasons (axe murderer, death by sea, instant love affair, bewildering loss of memory?). I could go on, of course, but will not. Even if he came back years later, I'd hate him for it, having come to terms with his brazen departure years ago. Also true: I felt a pang of relief that he had finally gone, after so many false starts, leaving me to watch the skies.

And in the end it all boils down to, all boiled up to, a figure of grandiloquent nothing. All the same, no matter who had seen it, the same pregnant zero, with no one on board save the shadow of a camera wholesaling the image of humanity back across the galaxy to never-never land.

All very well, unless Earth is the only "civilization" with any human life at all, no matter how bloodthirsty (apart from the several second glitch of peace back in the twentieth century). Not very impressive to Alien eyes. Bypass, back to the song of the Earth, granted the status of also-ran on account of their habit of boiling children alive.

I adopt this telegraphese mode of reporting to give my prose a clinical lift, nothing like the presumed language of courteous refinement which will replace us when we are gone, felled by the unstoppable cannonball of some cosmic event. Some pith at the last, unlike the mellow periods I am normally given to.

Bang, crash.

Enter the Aliens, after a long wait.

All speaking conventional English, the tongue long denied them.

And so it goes, until the next cosmic detonation.

Long enough to let the Aliens hate one another, to get to warfare's clammy grip. What a waste of gift and intelligence, like Lomax himself, the self-waster.

Time repeats itself until the next Alien civilization, all the books and artworks of the previous two generations gone to naught. Too gloomy to endure.

I would give a lot to see thousands of Aliens coming in to land, talking among themselves for the first time, setting up shop in any ruined pitch-black relic. A new start, by a race much in advance of ours, never to be seen (of course) by ourselves. Plunking down their sandwich-shaped obelisks.

"'Ave a sandwich, mate."

"Don't mind if I do."

They go separate ways, chortling of their newfoundland.

It would not be like that at all.

It would protract the long, unendurable silence, broken at last in a new century. Not one of us would be alive to witness it, not one of our numerous artifacts would remain for them to glimpse. Starting from scratch, light-years ahead of our ghosts, rapidly advancing.

I thought again of Lomax. No sign of him, not even of his henchmen. He, they, must be spending the nights together, I thought, at last surrendering to an old passion for gumballs or gimbals. I couldn't tie it down quite, but automatically assumed it had nothing to do with me.

As the days passed with no sign of him, I began to worry in my self-imposed role of gamekeeper. Had he at last found the Shangri-la of Shangri-las, committed to a new way of life, after a long and futile sojourn in the enforced company of a UFO believer? I wondered about him, especially about the wounded legs, asking myself if they were real or false, trying to decide from their angle or new shape what lay beneath. No good. He must have brought with him a goodly supply of bandages, so as to blind me with medical science. And I wondered at his posture in the wheelchair. Was it appropriate for a wounded warrior (an aerialist to boot, meaning one who thought he could fly)?

Nothing gained from all this blind cogitation. What of the gifts bestowed on the only too willing recipients, now reduced to a few fireworks, several outsize lollipops, some few spinning tops still in their disheveled wrappers (I peeked). That portion of his vivid, explosive life was shot, as was the day of the blithe parasailing. Instead, he had settled for a different life, closer to that of the Mongols, who treasured him along with his treasures (even when they stopped) and they found themselves stranded with a mechanical whale who kept them up all night with tales of epic feats of gliding, high over the mountains, low over the waves. A Genghis Khan of the sky, hoping to impress with sheer prowess, the UFOs a forgotten subject. Indeed, he had probably found my insistences on their woof and texture an insupportable tedium (not *te deum*). He seemed more at home with his boys and unlikely to return. Maybe some act undivulged so far in his rake's progress between heroism and shame would classify him as a hero finally, whether the last act depended on reckless folly or immortal disgrace. Then he could relax, knowing he had given his all, to Chernobyl or the Ides of March, and no more would be demanded of him, not in this life anyway.

SIX

The more he stayed away, the more I eased my limbs, took my repose with increasing sleep, and began to shed the waking dream of him, a lost and unmourned mountebank, reborn of foreign parts. By the same token, a recalcitrant chunk of my brain worried about him with the last shred of my overfed conscience. What had happened to him? This was a question from a curious observer, asked in the usual demand for *information*. Information, as if it would do us any good in the hereafter.

He had taken up with a curious sect.

He had foresworn all parasailing.

He had simply tired of me and my hang-ups.

He had kowtowed to an enemy and warlords joined his band.

A heaven-sent fatigue occupied the intervening days, sparked by too much wondering and too little sleep. Then I pursued the ghost of Lomax, uphill and down dale, all to no purpose. It may not have been the biggest of towns, but it was big enough to strike terror into the heart of comparative busyness.

I asked little and got nothing in return. No sign of him or them, which is not surprising when you consider the language barrier, both ways, even with the police, whose energetic compassion only made things worse. One man missing plus at least three hangers-on made a wonderful combination for anyone seeking company, but not for anyone hunting the lost.

Oh, the helpless attitudes that confronted me as I got to grips with my problem. Not only had Lomax not been seen, maybe he had never existed, and I had been dreaming the whole enterprise, from hussies making inroads on our sexual privacy to the full blast of his departure and eventual return with wounded joints. Lomax was as invisible as one of my Aliens, and just as contented to be so.

I suspected the police of flagging in their endeavors, pushing Lomax to the brink before edging him out of sight as one of the forgotten, (remembered, if at all, by a white-haired eccentric who should have stayed at home). What did the police think about? Drugs and little else. The jails were already full anyway, with scores of contenders awaiting the next vacancy. This apart, the police were a posse of gravelly-mouthed, fresh-faced lads who needed employment. In other countries, they would have been out of work from birth until doomsday.

There was nothing for it but to spur myself on, concentrating on the likeliest places: the bus terminal, the ladies of the dark infested places where a hand job cost little, the taxi stands—even the taxation office, full of the wretched who had come to plead their case. In fact, I found it difficult to distinguish the likely from the unlikely, the two joining hands across the Gobi Desert in a sandstorm of grit. Where next?

My search by taxi slowly expanded south, I knew not why, down past the minor airport at Mandalov, further down past the 300,000 year-old human skeleton, as far as the ancient rock paintings called Ulaan Suvagre, finding my way back, and thence to the airport quizzically dubbed Home. A long sortie, which apart from sore feet and sardines filched from Lomax's remaining hoard of goods, was an exercise in peripatetic boredom and sullen mind.

Next, a less fatiguing trip to the north, outskirts only, to find what? I had already lost hope. Most of my friends were already dead (popping off their perches like ninepins), and in any case Lomax was becoming less than friend, a blithe irritant, rather, his human quality receding fast as light. Still, however, perhaps to be found.

What came next had a spellbinding quality like being burned alive, slowly. As if I'd thought of it in the first place (I hadn't thought of it at all), I addressed myself to the newly built, pepper spray red Genghis Khan Hospital, on the slight slope next to the Gandantegchilen Monastery, a place as unpronounceable as all the others, designedly so (I thought) to keep foreigners away. Truth told, locals reduced the word-order of its title to sound like "Goodchildren," making it available for all and sundry.

Maybe the portmanteau name had been enough to keep me away, which was why I first tramped through steppes and rock gardens, through tourist areas and mineral water springs, to find my friend of old. But once the hospital announced itself in a friendly way, I had approached it, all awnings and muslin to get one in the mood before they got to grips with pincer and saw.

At first, my view was cynical (another place to visit in vain), and then myopically attentive. It must have been something in the air, a strange blend of peppermint and senna, the one countering the fetid smell of the other. On the second level, I noted a warmth missing from the floor below, and I began to relax my vision. Another wasted trip, I thought.

And then I saw the ghost of him, legs swathed in bandages, face, as usual, stained as if bleached, with eyeholes rimmed black, the whole suggestive of some nightmare recently borne with great courage. His eyes were closed, somehow clenched tight as if defending against something external, and his arms looked withered and sunken. He had lost pounds, and I shied away from inspecting his feet.

He opened one eye, whispering, "I thought you'd come sooner or later." And in explanation: "Chernobyl, catching up with me at last."

I gaped, prey to several conflicting emotions, and eventually said, "How's it going?"

"Can't you tell?"

I could, but said nothing.

"I feel spavined."

"You ought to be back home," I said ambiguously.

"No fear."

"You look old to me."

"To you and who else?"

It was not going well, this shapeless conversation with a dying friend, who had gone tramping the poisoned steppe, God alone knew why. To achieve this. A nurse intervened, pleading his radioactive belly. "Please to go." It was the first thing said to me by a native in English. I almost wept.

I let myself be ushered back, down two floors into the chockfull, noisome waiting room smelling of infected spittle and the brittle breaking of miscellaneous wind. Then I walked out into April sunshine, glad to be free, but tense with worry about my friend, his complex, bewildered motives and his chance of surviving. Too far gone, in my estimation. A month or six. Why had I not visited the hospital before this? I would not have been much good to him, counseling him about his unworthy henchmen, and failing to advise him about his disease.

As I checked my pace, feeling truly wretched in spite of the abundant sunshine, bizarre and evasive thoughts entered my head, anything to feel less abandoned and puny. If he had only taken more bee pollen with his micro-algaes, he would have felt better. This would have helped with the gastronomic chaos in his lower belly. He looked like a celiac victim, white dung pouring out of him like cement.

In truth, there was nothing I could do to help him. He had received many times the fatal dose of radiation during his short stay within the radiation belt, and god alone knew where that ended or began. The attentive, brusque Russian guard had not intervened soon enough, merely having made his rounds in the normal way. A half-minute more would have delivered Lomax a fatal dose, instead he was given a year before it plunged deep into his vitals with no hope of reprieve.

Clearly, his legs had been affected, he having always exposed them, knobbly or not. Something to do with sunlight and sufficiency, although I doubted, with the monster of radiation to be reckoned with, that it would have made much difference whether he was swathed in lead or baring knees to Chernobyl's winds. The monster, as I had begun to call it, must be appeased, and that was that. There was no halfway house in dealing with it. He was bound to die, like thousands of volunteers conscripted in the obedient Russian way, who had condemned themselves to a permanent agony after only half a minute's exposure.

On the whole, he was remarkably cheerful in his doom, wincing periodically as the monster sunk its teeth into him, leg, bowel, or arm.

"What's the pain like?" I had impudently asked him during one of the slack moments of our long postponed interview. "Does it hurt badly?"

He paused before responding, "A dull form of acid," he pronounced, "Varying from a sharp razor to a blinding apoplexy. That should cover it."

It did. What did he mean by apoplexy? Wrong word? Or an almost lost meaning revived for the emergency? I postponed the question for later as I sank into comfortless oblivion, having left another of my friends behind me along with Hawkes, Mann, Young, Hargreaves, Rees, Bolton, Davis, Tall, and the rest. I had been reserved for a larger, ampler fate, right here in Mongolia, perhaps. I found time to ask him about the respective fates of *Nugas, Tarvag,* and *Bodon G.*, but he had no answer, and I assumed they had gone the way of all flesh, alert for their bright shining moments, then plowed under like so many earthenware embryos.

Having finally found a secure footing amid the lumps of clay (the hospital was a new thing, not yet groomed to elegant surfaces), I found my way home, and wept my fill, having misjudged my friend. Then I ate a slice of fierce cheese, which restored my aching spirits somewhat and prodded me to further action—or would have done so if I had only known what to do. Nothing for him. Nothing for them, wherever they were. Nothing for me. Having done all that hiking by taxi in pursuit of someone five minutes walk away, I finally settled for sleep (4:12 pm), reckoning it better to still the mind before resuming the impossible.

The darkness began it, starting with my own father's special darkness: the tint of his black shoes, the furry black of his shoelaces, black socks and black tie. I plunged into these memorabilia like a bridegroom looking for solace, aching to find a dimension that ruled out Light Lomax's pallid, infected face. It was not black enough, so I deserted my father (if such a thing was ever possible) for things blacker than night, smothering with pitch, choking me with black-letter stamps, anything to shut out the hideous image of his descent into the dark. It was not a bad idea, this using dark to shut out light, except that its spatter betrayed me as not dark enough, and left my facile importuning in the dust: gray, gray-black, fuliginous something or other. Not quite black enough for me, who wanted something that shut out his face completely, with nothing to tell you where face left off and dark began.

I began to hallucinate, using black to simulate an extreme of color that did not exist. It was, in the idiom of the old astronomy classes, a soft, subdued, nonassertive gray, with always something seen against a matte black background, shining like hope for a quick redemption. Or with the black-body radiation peeping out from behind the rest, always something to cheer you up, to get you off to a palatable start lest you surrender to total blackness and never hope again.

That sort of opacity. Later on, I realized I wanted to be rid of his face entirely, too much for one to bear who had grown accustomed to its jovial pink, a face that wrinkled a thousand ways with, all the time, an expression of hail-fellow, well-met. I wanted his beloved face, his chops and throat to merge into the mighty *never* where all painful expressions die. Then to be gone. But his physiognomy lingered on, mutely protesting the ignominy it suffered daily, a cheapening of expression here, a withering away there, never joining forces but always distorting as first one determined cell decided never to move again, then another beefed up its effort and produced a new twitch, painful and ghastly.

He really did not know what his face would do next, not to mention the rest of his body. He was all expectancy, gearing himself for the next twitch, the next spasm, yet being capable of ducking it, so his life had been rendered a brute of torsion, with thousands of minor movements all directed to making him feel another fraction worse. Slowly, inexorably, the chemical reactions ate him away, night and day, until the time when it would end: meal complete, but still going on after death, in the manner of such greed.

No wonder I sought, in vain it must be said, an anodyne for all this suffering—a quick release of it all, a crescendo of unimaginable blackness that included me along with him. Things did not work that way, ever, and I was alone, consuming my rice and broth, my Jodhpur lentils, my mess of pottage until the last trump sounded. I vowed to visit him each day, watching him slowcoach away, first racked this way, and then that, until he ceased all motion while his body continued to clean up after him, obeying its slave.

He and I used to say sometimes of unfortunate events, *Absinthe* makes the heart grow fonder (or stronger), but more in gratitude for having found the pun than for anything spine-shattering, or knee abolishing. What had happened to Lomax was the epitome of disaster, the whole of it perhaps as yet unread (those legs). To go back, as I did, unraveled further misadventures.

Not a piece of him had survived intact. He was as I used to say *spavined*, which meant ruined from the neck down, and then some. Had he stayed in position there among the last fling of snow, punishing his body little by little, if at all (he was an expert skier and more than competent at freshwater rafting). Or if he had kept out of Chernobyl—as millions had, content to roam the Southern Seas—all would have been well. Or, if not well, only partly injured, soon to spring to life again.

But it was useless to speculate about the legs, just as useless to ask—which reminded me of a long treasured Latin tag that began "you ask me to repeat unbearable things," or something like that. (At last, my Latin is slipping away from me, a treasure trove instilled by a Mr. Somebody who perished in the 1943 war, but not before bestowing on me the gift of tongues.)

I assumed the worst. No legs left. What I saw was most diligently wrapped, purely for effect, as if to calm the legless. Maybe, one day soon, I would be legless too, or without arms, buttered up to prolong the dreary amputee's dream of paradise. I had noticed in myself a ribald insinuation of cock-a-hoop joy, in which I soldiered on, come what may. Legless, armless, I'd determined to prevail until the last trump sounded and the headmaster pronounced the fatal formula at last: "Down toys, gentlemen. It is over."

It was not, not yet. I sped to Lomax's bedside and found him in the throes of leg-binding, an experience fortifying and soft, for he was without his toes (frostbite or marcescence). I was too intimidated to ask questions. If I waited long enough, I needn't ask at all. There I stood, not invited to sit down, staring at the blunted tips: no nails, severed at the root, and distilling upwards a keen aroma of shorn horn.

It was an amazing sight, the toes as if the space they had occupied was making way for something else, larger and longer. I stared it down at last and seated myself unbidden. To say that he emitted howls of pain during this procedure would be too much, but in their place he substituted suffering motions that occupied his entire warped body, as if he had been condemned to the garrote, one screw at a time, winding its way through with complacent ardor. I felt so helpless. His pain resonated inside me.

Finally the foot-binding was finished. He sank back into the pillow, a man pushed beyond his limits, and began to talk in falsetto overtones about Chernobyl, the human wastage of those condemned to Mother Russia. I listened, appalled.

SEVEN

That heavily irradiated zone north of Kiev had at least one surprise in store. It had become one of Europe's biggest nature sanctuaries, with, for instance, the famed wild Przewalski horses grazing the exclusion zone around Chernobyl as if nothing had happened. Wolves, lynxes, deer, moose, and wild boar. The bad side of all this natural wonder was that all were radioactive with Cesium-137 and Strontium-90 invading their muscles and bones. In spite of this, they thrived. All but brown bears, which had disappeared.

Not bad, I thought, for a massive area forbidden to humankind. Poor for Light, excellent for animals and some birds. Chernobyl was a paradox all right. How to sacrifice an old friend on the altar of a radioactive Przewalski mount? Some days, I was turned away from my daily visit (patient not doing too well) and became a prisoner of thought. How long could he last like this? Was there no way of making him right? Alas, no, once the ravening beast has you, he has you for good. In the stupefied condition I found myself in, I dashed off a wire to the people back home, explaining the situation as best I could.

I noticed that my permitted visitations were alternating: yes, no, yes, no, always the same, and I concluded they were shielding me from him, never mind his status. I remonstrated, but it was no use. They would not let me in until the next day, and so as time passed I divided my days into *think* and *visit*, yielding to some weird alternation in my heart, which rigorously kept the zones clear of one another.

Did this mean, therefore, that I kept visiting days, when I did not think (I deplored, I empathized), and on thinking days I committed myself to abstraction? I tried, but the days kept spilling over into the other, hardly able to tell the two apart. Which was easier? Neither, and I was amazed at my mental naiveté in proposing any such idea. Truth told, I was ashamed of my previous rotten conduct, assuming this or that to his constant detriment when all the time he was suffering the torment of the damned nearby in the hospital.

There was nothing for it but to make up for lost time, showering him with unnecessary gifts (pipe-cleaners, boxes of chocolate, comic books), none of which were relevant to his ever worsening condition. You have to give *something*, come what may. Most of the time we spent in ritual sighing, he always first (with an exasperated snort), mine more like a baby's with a cold. We waited for the moment of speech, but it rarely came, just a few syllables about comfortless positioning or thanks for succor. We had come past the moment of speech, self-restricted to an imperfect sign language of the heart, past which there was no going.

No wonder I doted on the little verbal exchanges that we mustered between us. These were the *last words* we would exchange, so let them be true.

By the time of the next *yes*, with me bright and early (9 am), he smelled worse, this time of ammonia. I reported this to the duty nurse, but she shrugged it off as par for the course. He was not expected to get better, she said. He was expected to get worse, and to smell accordingly. This was not good news, but hardly a surprise. My old retrieved friend was going downhill, and I could do nothing to help. He was not sensible of his condition, though from time to time permitting himself a woebegone, half-paralyzed smile that bespoke the full measure of his suffering. He was looking forward to the end, I thought, not like a bridegroom entering his chamber, but like a man to be hanged making love to the rope.

And who could blame him? One folly at Chernobyl, and all was lost. By all accounts, he was just nodding off to sleep when disturbed by the ranger (or whatever he was). All too late. If he had slept, his condition would have been worse. Why had he chosen to sleep there, inside the exclusion zone? He did not remember, and now he looked a mess of half-strangulated pottage, his body an unbecoming mauve tint, sign of corruption and radioactive waste.

Was I indignant? Almost to the point of speechlessness. This being had trekked enormous distances to see me a second time, and here he was, his effort blighted, and to hell with the three hangers-on who had curried his favor. They had deserted him now, not that he had ever needed them, except as by-play during several dull moments.

He stirred a little, groaned with interior pain, and then, as it were, lived with it since there was nothing else to do. God grant the pain did not become worse as he neared the end. They had fed him an anesthetic, but what could you reasonably expect from nurses in the middle of nowhere, baffled by what they were treating? He was alone with his pain, like all the other poor Chernobyl residents who had gone before. Tales of splendid, contaminated, wild horses meant nothing to him. He would have sentenced them all to strontium-cesium death in seconds, could he only survive.

He groaned again, faster than usual, as if the pain had reached crescendo, renewing the first hurt before the previous one had had its way with him. I argued with his day nurse that had I been allowed to visit him daily instead of alternate days, he would have fared better. No use blathering with those hens of the deep country. They said no to whatever I proposed. So I made light of his groaning, teaching myself to regard it as normal practice, the sound of a sleeper plunging himself into an even deeper slumber. That way I could endure it, the feral growl that degenerated into sudden desperate yelps of pain beyond comprehension.

Soon he would be silent, overcome by his old assassins, strontium and cesium. Better say what had to be said beforehand, but what to say, with Lomax semi-consciously groaning assent to whatever I said. He was beyond language already, except for moments of plain speaking limited to requests for change of position or reshuffling the bed (which was primitive and not freshly laundered). Would he have fared better in one of those *de luxe* suites in Washington, with nurses scurrying to help and urgent doctors at his beck and call? I doubted it.

It did not take me long to establish my way of cheating the either-or system of the hospital. On the forbidden day, the *no,* I presented myself and addressed lavish care on everyone but Lomax, in fact scrupulously avoiding even looking at him. In this way I endeared myself to all the battered and bleeding (without, need I say, deciphering a word of their speech). In time I had become Yank to all and sundry, and the nurses simply could not bring themselves to deny me access to my old friend, though he mainly slept through it all. I sweetened the pie with boiled sweets (mostly sugar-free Starlight Mints, this red and white striped booty stolen from what was left of Lomax's hoard).

In a short time, I had the run of the building, both floors, and my supply of candies had run out (replenished by bogus Mint Imperials, sold in a little shop devoted to Imperial Preference). But by then, Lomax's condition had not improved, and he spent hours of stertorous sleeping with intermittent bursts of semiconscious pain, which I was powerless to prevent. The nurses fed him intravenously, sometimes holding his hand or forcing bread down his throat (the local method of cure).

What attracted me when I first noticed it, was an array of tiny lights in a courtyard, which mimicked a train of sorts, which shuddered about, then took off, disappearing around the corner of the building. It moved leftward, encountered something like a bump, and then climbed at an angle of forty-five degrees.

At first I thought a car, then a hydroplane, a helicopter. It always started with a buzz, then traversed leftward space before ascending. I never saw it coming back, though it would reappear suddenly without seeming to move through the intervening space. I started sneaking back to the hospital in the small hours to study it. Where did it go, and whom did it ferry in the dark, and for what? I became a midnight gazer, with the world asleep, I cast my eyes on the vital corner where all the action was. Was I imagining the whole thing, or was it real? No one else seemed to have noticed it, the quiet shuffling of its gait, increasing speed as it went.

Was I at last losing it? Maybe overconcentration on the illness of my friend was paying me back in full. Sometimes, the train (whatever it was) stood there for hours, erratically blinking its lights. At other times it chortled forth on several expeditions within a quarter of an hour, always returning to the same place.

What in daylight proved to be a common or garden array of windowpanes, turned up at night as a mysterious willow-the-wisp, ferrying (I presumed) unknown people to magical destinations. I poured over its woof and texture, eyeing it as I had once eyed my friend, hoping to track the thing down to its point of origin, the point where it vanished only to return. Let's face it: my attention wandered each night from my doomed friend to this captivating, fickle apparition, perhaps sent to divert me from my funereal task.

Sometimes the train changed direction, omitting the bump or even the second skyward lunge. But never lacking the first leap, which proved *de rigueur* throughout the night as I stood patiently watching. Sometimes the muted explosion of setting off was bigger than usual, I didn't know why. Suffice to say, as Lomax dwindled before my very eyes, occasionally requesting a slice of bread or renewal of his anesthetic, my response to the as-yet-unnamed (and perhaps unnameable) apparition took flight, domesticating it with a mother's zeal, coying up to it by night, coming to depend on it in all its variations.

That it was meant for me, and no one else, seemed axiomatic to me. No one else needed it, so I unhesitatingly began to relate it to my friend's sapped condition, linking its friskier moments with his, and his somnolent doldrums (much more numerous) to his possession of what I had begun to call his sleeping quarters. It was a risky procedure, this co-opting of a machine to a human being, breathing his last, but I did, lacking anything else to do during the passive hours of his silence (daytime) and the excited intervals of the machine (night).

I tried hard to devise some name for the machine, but this for some reason evaded me. Perhaps I shrank from the intense objectification of Light Lomax, as compared to any machine, especially one of changing personality and daytime invisibility. No one had seen it, but then I had no one to ask about it. Maybe thousands *had* seen its devious nighttime forays and had dismissed it with the same breath, relegating it to just another of the Jules Vernian spirits of prismatic nature, best left alone to ply its trade among human kind.

The machine was mine, my radioactive friend less so. If he recovered, things might be different, but there was little chance of that now, with the nurses making lugubrious signs above his head, and with the complete relaxation of all the visitation laws. *Visit when you want.* As for the machine, no one had ever observed it, as their faltering English made plain. They did not know what I was talking about. Still less, when I resorted to sign language; they attributed the dumb show to an American trick not to be taken seriously. I suspected them of wishing my friend dead, rid of the two of us in one fell swoop.

Imagine my consternation, when I was visiting the hospital two days later. For the first visit, he was there, for the second, not, and I at once suspected a nurse of muffling his breath with a pillow to ease the problem of the crowded wards. Far from it. He had just taken the opportunity to walk away, with his wheelchair, of course. He could not be found. The TV made its customary appeal, but he had up and left, just like that, in his hospital clothes, a fatally escaped man hurrying towards his maker with all possible speed. He could not have gone far, and I expected him back by nightfall.

During the next couple of days, I observed the police requirements concerning missing persons and contemplated his absence—a few boxes of boiled sweets left gaping open, two multicolored neckties (never worn, not in my memory of him), and some never-to-be washed again bandages intended for a certain pair of injured legs. Who *was* he after all? A loyal friend, point proven, but still a hanger-on, prey to flattery and inimical to UFOs. I may have been harsh in my dealings with him and his main acolytes *Nugas, Tarvag,* and *Bodon G.,* but I made up for it with my persistent hospital visits and my treks by taxi over the length and breadth of Mongolia.

On the whole, I preferred his previous incarnation to his most recent—the ebullient Lomax of doxiedom to the wheelchair bound of the hospital. But you can't have everything your own way, and I certainly did not fancy his latest embodiment of missing: believed killed or near to death in some barren location, so fearful of death he decided to speed it up.

I could hardly ask his whereabouts, not having the language available, but I attempted various modes of dumb show, miming wheelchair and disappearance, much to the pleasure of bystanders, who did not have the faintest idea what railed me. A pleasant guffaw trailed behind me as I made my walk from pillar to post. Obviously, he cut a dramatic figure, but they could not connect him with my fumbling histrionics.

In despair, and having heard nothing from the police, I returned at dusk to his old stomping ground, second floor at the hospital, to see if he had returned unbidden to his last place of rest. No such luck. His bed was already occupied by a coughing old man, soon (I could tell) to be occupied by another patient.

I interrupted my grief and frustration by staring at my recent find—the train, helicopter, or whatever it was that plied the curtains of the night with curious motions, going out and returning invisibly during the hours of darkness. Nothing had changed. The same arrangement persisted, but I noticed (for the first time) that the engine reached crescendo before taking off on its limited excursion. I also noted how, sometimes, it steepened the angle of its climb, twice, and then lay apparently dormant for hours.

It was high time I named it. Then I could find Lomax, wherever he had holed up. This was a risky idea, index to a desperate state of mind, mocking the very notion of radiolocation (or whatever). He could be found by magic alone, or so I reasoned, other sources having let me down.

It did not work out that way, however. The little train plied its traffic through the night, with my headachy self behind it, going without dinner just in case, but retiring finally with no success. The preposterous notion that came next to me, perched in my nightshirt in his unoccupied bed, was that he had just taken the train, with its puffability swoop, and then gotten off in the acre of tenement that flanked the hospital, never to be seen again.

Strange to say, things began to come together for me, with Lomax missing, the UFOs silent as ever, and the twinkling machine ferrying out to no discernable purpose. I was rapidly devoting myself to nothing, but hugely so, still expecting at any moment him to reappear, the UFOs to find their voice, and the machine to find its purpose.

Not exactly a satisfactory complement, but one that would do for the time being, taking its form from the active world as a friend retrieved, a voice found after a long wait, and a machine finally given its purpose.

Many a life, I persuaded myself, chugged to the end without finding any such purpose. Perhaps the fate of most lives, waiting for something that never happened, never produced its voice, never completed itself. I was making do until something superior turned up to brighten my life, but it was something to hope for in the midst of gorgeous Mongolian sunsets.

You had to have a little tincture of imagination to greet the overflow when it arrived. Stands to sense, I told myself. *Eric, or, Little by Little,* I said, remembering a children's book of long ago. I was discovering the part played by next to nothing in the human equation, not jubilantly, but with a sense of something just barely accomplished where there might have been nothing. There was never *nothing.* You could rely on that, so it was vain to worry about the void when all the time there was something to worry about. Of the something's fragmentary nature, hardly perceptible, let nothing further be said, beyond its not being expected to make whoopee. I was accustoming myself to the little that was available, shortening my sights before being overwhelmed.

You can play such mind games forever, for a comparative season anyway. Not for you, talk of black or white holes in space, or the magnetosphere, or Einstein-Rosen bridges, if you believe in such fol-de-rol. I serenade the minute thing missing, then found. Or continuing the parable of incompleteness never found, like the source of our universe. I suppose that includes such mysteries as Bent Water, Sag Harbor, Roswell, The Brazilian Roswell, and Area 51, but no matter. Such things are sent to infuriate us out of our minds, when we should be living with them, rejoicing in their enigmatic presence.

It may be hard to say it, but the disappearing should be allowed to be absent without leave. And all the rest of what Sam Beckett called the "morbid dread of sphinxes." Sphinxes should be let in, to scald and terrify us, just for a change of horrors. What is worse? Being condemned to death by Hitler or being confounded by a sphinx?

Coming down to earth again, I wondered about wondering. Was it worth it? Why not live opportunely amid the babble, letting it rain down upon us? Live with it—approaching reverence even? Such thoughts, necessarily incomplete ones, occupied me more and more, so that much of my life (what remained of it), became a salute to the demon of things let loose because there is nowhere else to put them. This solved the problem of Lomax in a trice, conferring upon him a perhaps unwanted liberty.

The next event was a nonevent. No sign of Lomax, but everyone had seen him ages ago, perambulating by wheelchair down narrow alleyways, rather than the arid wastelands to which I and my taxi committed ourselves, as our scope widened and our search became more desperate. Seen him, but to no purpose! The local language barrier discouraging most foreign interchange.

So, they *had* witnessed him, dispensing toy bugles, chocolates (white), and miniscule booklets (guides to the United States and other countries). But without talking to him, or at least without being understood. What a world to live in, all jabbering away in incomprehensible tongues, all the more reason for the UFOs to keep their distance. No mention of the three hangers-on: *Nugas, Tarvag,* and *Bodon G.,* subsumed in the irresistible glamour of his bedridden personality. It made a great deal of sense to find the three of them, overlooked as part of the mainstream.

Having seen him, hampered as he was, they should surely have remembered more of his bandages. But, no, he was relegated at once to the clutter of momentary spectacles that assailed the eyes of onlookers. Vivid for a moment only, then lost even among the *tohu-bohu* of Mongolian passersby. What on earth did they remember? Nothing that could be communicated. A rosy face and unkempt leggings? No, not even a loud preemptory voice "verging" nonetheless on sometimes falsetto, and a passion for ice cream (pistachio, mango).

Not the putrid bandages, or the scent of the German bread they periodically forced down his throat, or the snoring with which he adorned the neighborhood—a brittle throat-fungus akin to gazpacho. A man's shadow had passed them by and gone on to even more forgettable feats somewhere in China or Indonesia. I labored nonetheless to find him, just a shred of him, making him more memorable all the time, even fabricating characteristics not really his to make something indelible of him, and ending up with a total stranger whom in the end I prided myself *not* to know.

Ah, Lomax, the unrecoverable, the strayed lamb of our flock. Disappeared, as usual, and probably by now almost dead in some hovel or rat trap, having streamlined his end.

Expert as I was becoming with nonexistent forms, I was at a loss divining him, he who had so recently passed by me on his way out of the world. No farewell—he had gone so far into nonexistence as to supplant the need for that. The faceless goodbye was more his style anyway, at least the one he might have addressed to me. So I spoke to myself increasingly, making up for lost time, not finding attractive words to state my predicament better than, "Here's a nice how do you do" or, "It stands to reason." My ploy fishing for like with like, casting a shallow line in hopes of catching a shallow response. But no luck. He had disappeared like all the others, and I had a week ago added Rogers and Schneeman to the growing list. I would soon be the only one left alive.

And living forever, I had no doubt, basking in perfect sunlight and absolute event horizon, which to the layman means pneumatic bliss. In my time, I had sampled both, the perfect sun and the resilience of the sun after a long *Morketiden* which you acquire by intense dark longing, whether in a Mongolian yurt or an old Anglo-Saxon banqueting hall. It made me think of Genghis Khan, and how on his deathbed he had his retainers put to the block, and then their successors, just to enjoy a perfect paradise of uninterrupted bones. No record of where he had been buried.

Such morbid, ecstatic thoughts had always pursued me, making me wish for a purer fate than the most recent one. The survivor leaps over the edge to fight again, maybe even Light Lomax would, somehow finding his proper duration with his last gasp and surviving to do battle in another realm.

One hopes for that, but the hope rarely comes. All death is final except for in the ancient religions that sanction renewal, being reborn as a mouse or a fox, a twelfth century man, or maybe a piece of litmus paper floating on the wind. I saw the Lomax of yesteryear coming to resurrected life as a snowplow or a pea, glad to be alive again and hunting for his old friend of the doxies, eventually glad to be denied pleasure and content to go as a snowplow or a pea to the end of time.

This is when, my ancient voice intoned, we separate the men from the boys, the boys who cannot take the abrupt cessation of all we love and adore and the men who are willing to take it on the chin. A sage said: *the moving finger writes, then stops forever.* All I asked for was that minimal fraction that permits us to keep in touch, even if only atomically, like a cabbage leaf keeping in touch with the Queen of England, or like a mollusk keeping in touch with Genghis Khan's grandson Kublai. Not asking for much. Anything to obliterate the fearful silence that follows us.

Nothing doing, says the Ancient of Days. *Not in the business of pleasing you. Make room for the next generation. You have had your ration. Now move on, as the laws require.* So Lomax was gone forever, not allowed even a moment's invigilation of a friend or a book, or a page or a paragraph, or even of a half-formed letter A in the body of a scrawl. *Extirpation* they call it, these masters, or to adopt the new coinage, *virtually.* No further word allowed but this, not even a feat of oracular imagination.

EIGHT

Understandably, I think, I retired from the fray for a while, since there was nothing I could do within the human grasp of things. Then I came back to life as soon as I recognized the presence of a new source of power within my slackening grip.

I asked myself if there were any other way of identifying Lomax. The hospital was clearly a dead end. The doctors understood what they understood, but no more. And the blissful trinity of *Nugas* (I thenceforth name him *Nougat*), *Tarvag*, and *Bodon G.* were nowhere to be seen, having retreated to a yurt in the wooly grasslands of the steppes. I marveled at such a performance, buddy-buddies, then nothing-at-all, not even in the arid streets of Mongolia. They had presumably had their fill of him, my old friend now missing, maybe truly on his last legs.

But I hadn't reckoned on the police, who in their pedantic, organizational way had been pursuing Lomax from afar, not finding him, but aglow with reputation for having found everyone else. When it was clear that the hunt was going nowhere they had switched signals and without much difficulty rounded up the mystic three, whom they tortured for the latest Lomax-a-gram. Local scholars told me this, glad to have something to say, individually reporting to me what ferocious torturers the police were—sometimes helping themselves to one of their number, who returned nail-less and several inches longer, or didn't return at all, after being quartered by horsemen, who sped off in different directions, pulling the victim apart.

Their pinched, saturnine faces welcomed me into the holy of holies with muted American references indicating British English. Why had I not met these gentlemen before? There must have been half a dozen of them awaiting me in the cool tile of the armory, and all declaring what sounded like a mispronounced version of *yewsguise*, which I took literally for its echo (*yousguys*). Their welcome was not frivolous; indeed it partook of a dead man's obsequy. "We have not found your friend," pronounced with a throaty mannerism suggesting phlegm: *ve avnot vrend*.

But, *ve av dis*, said their leader, a small burly man with receding hair and a peaked cap too big for him. They ushered me into a smaller room which smelled of blood (blood smells dusty, at least to me), and I could see why. Here, in a heap on the tile, lay *Nougat*, his dominant color dark red, with the bloodstain extending down to his fingers, which sat at unfamiliar angles, clearly broken and unfixed.

Wordlessly, they sped me into the neighboring room, where *Bodon G.* awaited us, his face distorted by virtue of being racked, and clearly unconscious. He wore the rack bravely, I thought, having been worked on for hours and would soon be dead, or at least unrecoverable. A third room disclosed *Tarvag*, his face lamentably bloated and dripping from the excessive waterboarding which had been dealt him.

I was to understand that these procedures were still going on and had produced nothing so far. "Because," I offered, "they don't know where he is." A judicious smile crossed their leader's face, indicating assent. And then a broader smile, which said the process goes on until one of the three (I quailed at his dumbshow of his American) *krakt* wide open. Was he saying *cracked* or *croaked*? Both probably. The treatment would continue through the afternoon and please would I return the next day for further news? I would, no doubt, despite staggered as I was by what must have been normal police procedure. This was how they passed their days? What lay in the other rooms, well tended, discreet bonfires turning miscreants into glue? Pol Pot with a vengeance, I murmured, glad to get out into the open air, which smelled of molasses and burning wood.

No use badgering the hospital, only five minutes walk away, or revisiting the light train which only worked at night. I strolled around, fending off gross memories of the three, then retreated to my afternoon pillow, there to dream away the truth about how my Mongolian rhapsody had turned out, a bloody fiasco which had begun so well.

It was a fitful sleep, if sleep entered into it. I kept waking up with memories of the three wastrels, each going his own way to perdition at the hands of a hard-boiled half-dozen tormentors. After the first agony, there would always be others, both severer and more ingenious. But if they did not know his whereabouts what use was the torture? The answer seemed to be that it was due them anyway, as in the days of Genghis Khan. With that unpromising thought I drifted off to a frightful slumber peopled by innocents whose hour had come.

When I awoke, it was faint dusk, always chillier in those arid climes. My first thought was that I should hasten back to civilization, where my comfy room awaited me with German blanket and ancient comforter. And stop going after an unfindable Lomax and the tripartite system of tortured *aides de camp*. Forget him and them forever. Yet I was too loyal to forget him and too much of a worrier to abandon the three, even though I was unable to help. The notion of helping in some way still attracted me, even if I couldn't see how to do it, with Lomax absent several times over and his hangers-on brutalized beyond belief.

At last I withdrew my conclusion, persuading myself that Lomax would only advance to another, more refined form of absence, just as absent as my almost forgotten Aliens, and the three ne'er-do-wells might well advance to another form of torture (especially if they really did not know his whereabouts). Such as, in their case, the Iron Maiden, the garrote, or the technique known as forced gangrene (or "wet"), which eventually would turn their limbs to mush.

I pictured their rotting legs liquefying and concluded it was just what they deserved. This degree of improvised hatred astonished me. Where did it come from? Why did I hate them so much after so little provocation? I hardly knew them, apart from my conversion of *Nugas* to *Nougat*, hardly one of the great sound-changes in human history. It was, I decided, the frustration of it all, the impractical nursing that preceded his disappearance, and the ignominy of the fruitless search.

That was the answer to my lack of sympathy for the three. If, after all this, he turned up again, able-bodied as in the old days, things might be different. I would march into the police station and emerge with their battered corpses, ripe for more gifts and trinkets. I wondered what had become of *Nougat*'s bugle in the harum-scarum of interrogation. It provided a convenient fixed point for the atrocities that followed, for the police were just getting warmed up.

The howls that went up during the next day or two upset nobody at all, not even me. They were getting what they deserved for failing to locate their sponsor and friend. I shrank from the details of their immolation, persuading myself that compared with the fatal evils of Chernobyl, they were having a picnic. The true sufferer in all this was my friend, late of the Chernobyl policeman's vigilant rounds, who had suggested in terms not polite that Lomax should move on before the radioactive pox hammered him quite. It was already too late, as subsequent events bore out.

Well, why not jettison the whole ship and head for home and beauty where the tulips and daffodils were beginning to flower? Something held me back. It must have been the off-chance of finding Lomax's worm-eaten body. Truth told, both the forms of parasite known as *Nais pardalis* and *Nais pseudobtusa* had already switched from asexual reproduction to sexual, such was the power of the radioactivity on the ground. Doubtless, even more catastrophic events would follow, so said Gennady Polikarpov and Victoria Tsytsugina from the Institute of Biology, Southern Seas University Sebastopol. How could you not trust them, she especially with a name that took me hours to write in my little black book of natural disasters.

The very thought of going home again to Buttermilk Falls and Ithaca's well-named Gorges struck me to the heart. I had no desire to go. Better to stay among the Frozen Chosen, as we used to dub our Presbyterians. Better to spend the remaining years theorizing about the silence of the UFOs and the presumed death of Lomax, even the shadow factory of the decorative shades that so entranced me at the entrance to the hospital. Better to hang fire in this way than wait for anything robust to declare itself. I convicted myself of having a grasshopper mind, "grace-hoper" to some.

Some would say I had my fill and would be welcomed home again. Some others would say I should have bargained for more, such as a final resolution to the Lomax mystery or to the accompanying puzzle of the UFOs, the ultimate fate of the three hangers-on, the true nature of the magical shadow box that so enticed me. At times, I would cheerfully have gone away from it all to Timbuktu or to Ultima Thule, just to free my mind.

I decided to stay the course, come what may, with my little assortment of sphinxes to puzzle over until the crack of doom. Something new would open up, of that I was certain. Someone else would arrive, somebody else would depart. Life was nothing but a juggler's rodomontade, aiming neither to please nor displease, just there to beguile us while we wait for the last act. In which case, what was the sense in moving?

With that settled (the grasshopper's vision of plenitude), I returned to my unsatisfactory broodings, waiting for the next thing to happen, as phlegmatic as that. But things remained much the same, and against my will I found myself thinking *this is it*. Lomax would never turn up, the three would be subjected to ever more punitive versions of torture, the condition of the UFOs would not change for several hundred years at least, and the shadow game at the hospital would stay put long after the building was demolished. I was reaching the last quarter of my allotted span, and someone else would take over the unfinished elements of the endgame. A long way down the road a terminal taskmaster would bring all ceremonies to an end before committing all the world to cinders. It was such a relief. No more Klaxon horns, no more motorbikes, no more thumbing buses, no more anything.

My search for Lomax now extended to the desert grasslands, plus a determined interview of all the taxi drivers. I awaited a daily message from police HQ, stamped in aspic on the ivory table next to a golden lamp that burned day and night.

Whoever tipped this missive was a senior cop, reserved for the big league of criminals, and not obliged to do his own torturing. I welcomed him into the fold with all the others. Soon there would be nothing left of *Nougat, Tarvag,* and *Bodon G.,* and then the police would have a field day, a celebration with colored flags and bare bones.

It never ceases to amaze me how much time humans exercise in planning what to do next, never mind what they have in mind to do down the road. They often do not advance beyond the planning stages, perhaps because it's all they have in mind. I understand this well, being one for ordonnance, preferring the same every day, and say, orange, rosewater and mint as flavors of the month, actually doting on the three and broadening them out in full, savoring the lemon hue of orange, the sallow finery of rosewater, the slightly acid value of mint, and so on.

Thus my *apologia pro vita sua,* begging all questions, forever squandering the precise in the vague, and hoping to get away with it because there are always more of us than of them. The prize always goes to the clear-headed ones—the exact and unyielding parasites of clear thought, to whom nothing remains ambiguous. Let's hear it instead for the tasty meat dumplings they call *bansh.*

Where was Lomax, everywhere and nowhere? What of the three wastrels? Racked to death. What of the UFOs? As ambiguous as I myself. What of the autistic ghost visible nightly in the annex to the hospital? Dunno. And of other things forgotten? Nix.

Through all my muddied evasions masquerading as thought, there stalked the bony invader called conscience, asking repeatedly about guilt, asking the kinds of questions to which all along I knew the answers. So all was not sluiced down the forgetting pool of memory, but lodged, demanding a hearing. So, briefly, I repaired my omissions, starting with Lomax the lost, which was enough to nudge me out on my taxi-rides again, hopeless but sticking to my appointed task, getting to know Ulan Bator as I never had before, learning scraps of the language (much *bansh*), and always trying to find him relocated in the hospital.

I hounded garbage dumps and abandoned trucks. When no good came of it, I reconnoitered the more expensive locales. He was truly absent, and he could for all I knew, be on his way home, despite his wretched condition. I imagined him in his parlous state, on the steep heights that reigned above Buttermilk Falls, a last trip before summer began. Or a last trip to Palm Beach before the summer heat set in for good and the hotels began tearing up the antique floorboards looking for termites. Or a fleeting (fleeing) glance at Kuala Lumpur, just to check on the local tigers.

Amazing how the mind produces mythical destinations. I barely expected to find him again in this world or the next, a puerile phantom of a man dead set on severing his contacts with reality.

Nothing worked, neither the fantastic nor the commonplace. He was gone, much farther than most people go, destined for R.I.P. or *An Angel Touched Him and He Slept*. Unusual for him to go out like this, this lover of the bizarre and the wayward, unless he had managed to find in his expletive-ridden way something so hideously eccentric that there was no way of latching onto it—except by accident, after which I, the seeker, would be subsumed along with him in the full disaster. I almost wished this to be true, to be rid of him finally and freed of my obsession with phantom entanglements, none of which paid off. (As yet.)

Fortunately, I forgave myself, and resumed normal Lomax hunting, though with plodding certainty he would not be found, even dismembered. In this way, I felled three taxis, and adopted a fourth: two were victims of slight collisions, the third despaired and refused to go any further, the fourth (which I proclaimed my last forever) was minus a side door and driven by an octogenarian funeral inspector who proceeded to jar me and him in a series of reluctant shudders which cut down speed to the minimum. But what were we looking for when we got there? *Where* was *there*? I settled back in the slow shuffling machine and made do with looking for nothing, at long last glad of it. This would be my last taxi to anywhere, and I vowed to return to my galactic studies the instant the corroded wheels touched the point of return.

Ah, but I was learning to speak the language, just a smattering of it, much of the time dividing my attention between *bi oilgoj bain* (I do understand) and *bi oilgokhgii bain* (I do not). The former was easier to say, although using it led to several crucial misunderstandings. Why had we committed ourselves to a nation of lummocks when there was Polish available to cut our teeth on, and Russian? The *exotic*, was the answer, and look where it had got us. I vowed, if I ever got out of this mess, to fall with a lover's impetuosity onto English and never look back.

The most preposterous thoughts that came to me in all of this had nothing to do with Lomax. I wondered how the Aliens were spending their time. Was there change in their world of silent hovering embassies surrounding our planet waiting for what: Human beings to turn their backs on sadism? The very thought of it deserved ridicule, as if humans were capable of, at long last, finding the philosopher's stone and beginning the start of a Golden Age. No matter how long the Aliens waited, such a miracle could never happen. The delights of brutalizing would never go out of vogue.

This left me with not much to think on. I wondered when I would tire of it and what I would replace it with—a phantom figment that only appeared at night? Hardly. Then cute memories of what life had been like in the old days, before the second coming of Lomax? Not a bit of it. I was living with my head turned backward, anxious to find something to hold onto. It was like white paper on a white desk, when you find to your dismay you have been writing half on target, half off, and all you can do to fix things is to exactly rematch your paper to the desk.

Gradually Lomax's image receded, held in place by fewer and fewer strands of sentimental yearning. Replaced, if at all, by images of the three being tortured or by my trackless progress along the steppe. Not much to think about, and not much consolation either. Is this, I wondered, what the end would be like, fragments of ideas as soon sapped as spawned? I made an effort to conjure his image, but it evaded my best efforts at wholesome reverie. A rib cage there, a partial foot here. I shrank from the rest of him, better to leave him cold and ruined. And if this were too bold in my imaginings of him, then so be it, it was better than his flimsy ghost.

Instead, I abandoned my attempt at the local dialect and concentrated on snippets of lived experience—from the old driver of my denuded taxi, to the gifts Lomax had plied his three cohorts with: the bugle, the German chocolates, the spinning tops. I must have been inventing some of these, but let that pass. Invention only weakened the image of the man. So long as I kept on the impersonal side, all was well, and I was capable of keeping the dismembered ghost at bay.

It happens in the bizarrest ways, an element of surprise, when you consider the job well done and, for the hell of it, wander back along the same route to see if you missed anything the first time. Not expecting much, but alive to the opportunity of making a discovery, you go back in rather a disheveled frame of mind, little knowing what has dragged you out there again to witness things which you have already seen. This half-measure does not promise anything celestial or even bright, but one persists with it in the hope of being more satisfied than ever with some trinket that, maybe, has for reasons unknown surpassed itself in human estimation. Not expecting anything out of the ordinary, but then the extraordinary happens, diamond from clay or contrariwise, blood from stone and you marvel at life's little shifts.

I had already been to the nineteenth-century rock drawings at Baga Gazaryn Chuluu, and the Gimpil Darjanaion Monastery, without going into the interstices of Khukh Bura Sum, the ruins of a tenth century temple, which looked even older than that.

All this by taxi, of course, which was systematically eating its way into my supply of strangely anonymous bills, bright in color (at least to begin with) then dwindling to a shade of pale pigskin as their denomination increased. It was only money, after all, though ennobled by being in memory of Light Lomax, lost somewhere in the desert I was looking at. I have never been able to sever things from their immediate perspective, men or women from their temporary vicinity, or bus tickets from the machine that spewed them out.

The ruins of Khukh Bura Sum (KBS to me, in a concise flash), settling into grassland, looked less impressive than their name. A heaped bump of subdued steppe, with tinges of gray, it wasn't much to look at, with ruins peeping out like dismembered hatchets given a last reprieve before becoming merged into the final mêlée. I had the old man wait with his taxi, and explored for myself, noting where the temple's ruins tumbled (and presumably remained), and in particular where they still assumed a shattered-looking formation, now couched in generality where there had once been a bell tower or an embrasure.

The smell was unlike that of the wizened gray steppe, and the place seemed more melodious, as if a softer version of the arid landscape had survived the intervening centuries. I honestly felt the mellowness of absent bells, which I quickly attributed to the souls of all the mystics who lay beneath. I was having a delicious morning of it and fast becoming a convert to the monastery ten or fifteen feet below. I had elsewhere regaled myself with rock pinnacles and mineral springs, "Mother Rocks" of refulgent beauty and 300,000 skeletons, but this, this was a novel sensation provoked by subdued luxuriance, by grazing on old memoirs, almost a waft from a childhood long since banned but reviving this late as a last gasp made its way past the throat and contributed a certain sweetness to the air above. How I inhaled this very moment, not cognizant of where it came from, but blessing it for its vernal uplift.

I poked around, disturbing rocks, pinnacles, fishing for God knows what, anxious to prolong the sudden sense of being made one with everything. I wanted the rocks and pinnacles to share my joy. Even the lapsed stonework contributed to my moment's ecstasy, crumbling to my touch and redistributing themselves in a trice. Maybe this was a magical place. Open to all, could they but find it. And thousands had. Millions over time.

The next thing that happened was astonishing. There, in the midst of my ecstasy, dug up by my probing, surfaced a piece of femur, fresh killed, jarring my ever-receptive senses and finally, exposing to light a huge bony trophy which I recognized.

Surely this could not be *his*, fresh cut and bleeding, dusty and strangely warped. But whose else? And where was the rest of him? I underwent some kind of a revulsion. There was a decorum to such things, and no amount of familiarity with war and other bestial things allowed this to happen. But, once I cooled down a mite, I knew it happened all the time. I thought back to my father, who had been lucky: wounded in two eyes, yet one only with long term blindness. This was different, one of

The Invisible Riviera

the mutilations forbidden by the Geneva Convention. When I had cooled off even further, I realized how wrong I was: this was how things happened in any civilized society, and lucky you were to escape with such an exemplary mutilation.

My own father, deemed lucky to have lost *only* an eye, would have agreed. Allowed either eye, he could have seen, right next to him in the trench, the murderous results of war, men barely recognizable and dead. Was this Lomax, then? If so, where on earth was the rest of him?

Nowhere, it seemed, as with naked hands I scrabbled among the dust and clay, anxious to find him alive. I found nothing, not even the fragged morsel of someone else's body, airing for all the world to see like a classic of war, left boneless and splay-legged for survivors to find. Was this all I was going to get, not even a corpse? Just a leg in the dust? Some sort of military emblem warning me not to expect anything else?

In my delirium, I packed the leg in old newspapers, which I found nearby, and prepared to descend the benign plateau which had sheltered him, thinking what a surprise this was going to give my taxi-man, whom I found asleep.

"Drive-on," I said to his somnolent face, and left him to collect his wits as he bumped over the unruly turf. At least I was going home with something. I dropped it off at the police station and said goodbye to Lomax, glad to start the career of his mortal remains in the hands of someone else.

"Who?"

"Lomax," I said. "My old friend."

"Alive or dead?"

"You work that out," I said with an asperity I did not mean.

"OK," they said, yawning, unpacking the paper truss with a nonchalant air. "We get a lot of these." I *think* that is what they said. At least I assumed as much. I was eager to leave although they leaned forward, tapping the ashtray of morning, as if they expected something else, a word of explanation which would make more palatable what I had brought in for their consumption.

Confronted with the bared bone, one would have expected more interest, even if only of the saintly ghoulish kind which professed to have seen it all already, and then some. But they saved their whoopees of scandalized amusement for who knew what, for Auschwitz or the latest works of Pol Pot. This augured in them a huge appetite for the grisly, ever in perfect supply on our planet. And their successors would certainly be just as lurid as they, still wondering why the Aliens kept their distance.

Too, they had cast a critical eye over me as I left my calling card for them to dismember later on. They had inspected me with a hostile if mute glance, which said *What has he been up to now, this god-botherer of a foreigner, ever pursuing the lost?* In fact, in their bedazzled way, they found me of more interest, critically speaking, than they did poor old Lomax's severed leg, already surrounded by midges and fleas. What had *I* done? Nothing, essentially. Just searching for the rest of Lomax. Maybe they were by now case-hardened, even the young ones, and I thought before leaving of the other meaning of *numb*. They waited around for something screaming *atrocity* to the winds before venturing on the nod that proclaims a worthy abomination.

Home at last, I vowed to make one more pilgrimage to the site, by taxi naturally, to see what I had overlooked in my excitement over the first find. I had a dismal foreboding that things would be going downhill from now on, Lomax lost forever and something else, me not excluded, provoking an extra sense of loss. In this, I was not mistaken.

Then there was tea, followed by coffee, both as strong as I could make them (and in the outcome rather sludgey and rank). Followed by some of Lomax's scotch, which got me off to sleep. A few nights' reprieve from all the hurly-burly of the yesterdays full of reverential servility and much tossing and turning.

So that was the end of it: highly unsatisfactory, with one limb, an absent body, and an unforgiving mystery of Chernobyl. It didn't make sense, but so little of human life does, no matter who is running it. I called it happy aggravation, but there was more aggravation in it than anything else. More like prefrontal lobe stew or any other mode of pseudo-academic dishes. I kept my strength up, what was left of it, on tinned beef and Tizer (an old favorite beverage exported to outer Mongolia for unknown reasons), largely because my former diet of Jodhpur Lentils had for some reason given out. The difference was that it was over. He was dead and no amount of coaxing could revive him. No, my lot, henceforth, would be called mass wisteria, with apologies to the French artist who coined the phrase.

I made a great deal of fuss in the assembly of my pills (we diabetics often do), three times a day taking care not to choke on the big rough pill I always saved for the end of the performance, having choked many times on its ungiving surface. Lomax had often reminded me, suggesting in his caustic way that listening to me choke was like listening to a hayseed in hell. What the hayseed, so slight an impediment, was doing there in the middle of my throat, he had never said, and I had never asked.

Came the early morning of the third or fourth day, during which I had wept, repined, cursed the unsatisfactory diet I was on, and longed for UFOs, or the phantom phaeton of the upper story of the hospital. Did not know what to do next so long as it didn't amount to much. Call it accidie (*akedia*) if such words appeal to you. They don't speak to me, so I called it *funk*, a better word because it evoked another, fiercer one.

My outer door cannoned open, followed by the bedchamber one. Men visiting me at six a.m.? I recognized the polished, noncommittal leader as he said to me in a perfect English he had not tried hitherto, "You are required downtown to answer certain charges. Please present your wrists." I was shocked out of my gourd, but mainly by his English, which he had been saving up for grand occasions like a child hoping to delight his parents on Christmas Day. No, something more sinister. Like a child hoping to delight them with exquisitely pronounced German.

"You what?" I was mumbling.

"Need to answer questions, sir."

"Questions?"

"You know, pertaining to your old friend, Lomax."

"Now dead."

"If you say so. Come on, sir, the wrists please."

"No fear."

"What was that?" he said to the wall, borrowing an old mannerism which made me feel eleven years old while he played aloof senior.

"I said, no fear. Fuck off."

That did it. He reverted to his native language and reaching over the bed, clapped my hands in cuffs that brought tears to my eyes. "Take him away," he said in time honored formula to his two cohorts.

Thereafter, I began my recitation of events leading up to Lomax's recent appearance, executed in the manner of as much bonhomie as I could muster, the semi-confident tone of someone who has done nothing wrong. I especially laid it on thick when describing Lomax's antics with his three horsemen of the apocalypse.

None of this surprised them, not even my tale of finding the leg and nothing else; all was written down in some arcane script by one of the flunkies. The finding also of a man on the Moon they received with the same placid lack of excitement, as I supposed with some surprise had become natural for space-age flunkies. Now how many men had trodden the moon so far? Two? Even I had lost count, as the moonwalk quietly slipped into the realm of known things. I remembered Borges' statement that of all the signal events during his lifetime the vision of men prancing on the Moon was the best. Wherever he was now, lying inert somewhere in Buenos Aires, he would no doubt have been surprised how moonwalks had become taken for granted. Better to die while the moonwalking was good.

As the reader will have surmised, I was going through the motions, nothing more, my mind as ever dreaming of something else, the intractable problem of the UFOs or the phantom apparition leaving the second floor of the hospital. In fact, I was only half-listening to the admittedly good English of the chief interrogator when he produced from somewhere a pair of gleaming new handcuffs and asked me to oblige.

"Oblige?" I asked in the tone of the maltreated mastodon.

"You have become a person of natural interest. Simple as that. Please."

Against my will, hardly believing what was happening, such was the politesse of his invitation, I succumbed, feeling this was a childhood prank, gone as soon as created. I did manage, though, to blurt "He was my best friend!"

"Quite so. It happens in the best of families," said the lissome interrogator, "we are accustomed to it."

They conducted me to a cell and left me alone to contemplate what on earth I had said to get me into this fix. Perhaps I had let slip my response to the three stooges, or my incessant searching for Lomax among the dunes. I could remember only half of it. Bad dream. I kicked myself awake, but with the same result. I felt like Trevor Howard, having given the mistress of some house a loaded revolver to play with (an echo of an otherwise forgotten movie). Next would come the shot, and the husband would fall, his troubles at an end.

They brought me a bowl of pestilential soup, which I drank nonetheless, having a dry throat. And then resumed my bleary account of the early morning's doings. What had I done wrong in all of this? Whom had I offended so grievously when I retrieved his amputated leg? Yet here I was, charged with an offense not as yet known, but likely to be a capital crime. The jail sounded empty, a study in the coldness of interior weather. Outside it was mellow, freezing in here. And I was the only malefactor. I tried to clear my flea-bitten throat, but it would not yield, delivering a load of phlegm with each rictus of my mouth. Clearly, I was in for the long haul, for doing something awful to my friend, but what? I tried to sleep, but my handcuffs prevented it, and I lapsed into a fitful fidget that would have done credit to the prisoner of Zenda.

How does one maltreat a best friend? What, after I had nursed him, did I do wrong? What escaped my notice? Nothing I could account for. I racked my brain, but could not locate anything serious beyond a complaint about the three henchmen; some objection to the length of his legs; and one or two fits of anger over his reading matter (nothing about the UFOs for instance). All the rest was innocent as sin, my constant probing of it led nowhere at all, and I could not sleep.

Is it any wonder, then, that I reverted to my old favorites, the disappearing string of lights that graced the second story of the hospital, only to reappear blurred and fuzzy a few moments later? Ideal meat for a migraine sufferer, except that I was in one of my migraineur's reprieves: clear, unimpeded vision all round. For once, the UFOs escaped my mental purview, too complex for the situation of being locked up for no good reason.

It was easy to lose count. Was this the second or third day of my incarceration, the second or third phase of the morning or the afternoon? I was soon reduced to a day or night decision, peopled three times a day by gruel, which came in a tin plate unwashed since the last meal, and therefore unwashed forever. It went perpetually unscoured, perhaps intended for the next occupant of this sleazy jail, a faint crust around the rim that bore the seeds of some drastic infection.

Thus the thoughts of a man unjustly punished, awaiting the next round of his sentence: bastinado or the rack, for reasons unknown. I soon found out, and I gave thanks for not having to wait too long. There is among us captives a fear of having to wait for torture, beside which the actual fact of being tortured pales in comparison. Call it the uncertainty principle by which you imagine *all* the forms of agony that await you, instead of the one or two you get. There stood *Nugas,* rubber suited, ready to begin: in his overeager hands the bastinado, ready to strike. So it was the feet after all which would bear the brunt: no rack, no electrocution, no waterboarding, no genital cut-offs, and (I thanked God) no raucous music. I was being let off lightly, or was this just the beginning, all the other tortures to follow in due course?

NINE

He strung me up, feet first until he had the perfect angle to strike me from. Then he began, gently at first, almost coaxing me into pleading that he advance into stronger measures and not keep me waiting. They soon came, and made me repent the thought of pleading with him. I almost fainted with the next blow, but he kept on, increasing the punishment until I fainted outright.

Then he began again, starting with a gentle love tap until he attained the full breadth of his orgy (with my feet by now bleeding and certainly scrupulously enlarged, could I but see them), whipping me till exhaustion claimed him and he ceased, pouring sweat. I began to see this would be the first of many such encounters, and I fainted again at such a prospect, too weak to attempt to bribe him to stop. One hour's pause, and then he came back, as wordless as before, this time belting my legs and shins with a new ardor which promised a dismal future.

To say that I hurt casts a mild light on the whole affair. I was a bloody mess addressing myself to Death. *Please take me*, I whispered. *Been here too long.* Nothing happened, a shower of water hit me, full force, in an attempt to revive me. I drank some of my own blood.

Then, just as suddenly, the torture ceased. Why? Why on earth a strong diet of rubber hose on me in particular, the nurse of men, the caregiver of Lomax, the hunter of his whereabouts throughout Central Asia? Any further dose of the same punishment could carry me over the brink, I thought, considering how weak I was to begin with. And why did they care where he was, anyway? What was Lomax to them? Or I?

And then I reconsidered. It would be a simple matter to cut off a finger each day, prolonging and extending the agony (or beginning with the toes), piling up the torment until I confessed? To what? A hatred of Americans, just that and nothing else, pulled into the police station to undergo the torments of the damned for a big fat nothing? I would report the goings-on at the nearest Embassy, and sit back and watch the results. Assuming the Embassy would do anything at all, having better things to do in the Mideast.

My heels were numb, my head ached, and the rest of my body was soaked with the pain of anticipation. I escaped at last from the repeated *why me's* and addressed myself instead to the inevitability that it was me all along, as it had been for years. No end but this, take it or leave it. For some reason, I went back to the image of Oxyrhynchus, who had devoured the penis of Osiris, ruler of the Underworld, who wanted it back in its right place. But whatever Osiris wanted, it was Oxyrhynchus who had devoured his precious trophy, and none other. The fatality of events took me over; this was how it was going to be, and nothing else.

Imagine my surprise the day after, as my blood-soaked feet caked and dried, when who should enter my hovel at the crack of dawn but *Nugas* with a sunny temperament, bearing a bowl of Jodphur lentils, to make up for my ordeal the previous day. I troughed like a madman, in spite of my bedraggled heels. He too was now speaking English, not perfect but better than nothing. He said: "Apologies for yesterday. He wanted exercise, and you were the nearest target."

I gulped at this, then concentrated on my meal, half-fearing that whatever *Nugas* said, this would be my last. Go down with a full stomach. How had he found out about my preferred dish, acrid and fierce as it was? I kicked the empty bowl aside and produced several shrieks of pain as he massaged my wounds. "My, I really laid it thick. Must have really wanted the exercise."

I gave up reconciling the torture of yesterday with the mellowness of today. Here he was, expressing sympathy, and I confess I waited for the first of the day's assault and battery to start, his cheerful demeanor notwithstanding.

If you have sore feet, you make a scuffy noise with them, in part afraid they are going to set about you once again once breakfast is over, this time breaking bones and making blood vessels pour until you faint again, begging not to wake. Surely though, his pleasant aspect would forbid any such performance.

Surely they would scourge someone else instead, someone who had made light of the president or some other luminary.

"How's the feet?" He sounded seriously interested.

I mumbled a reply, then thought better of it. Why stir them up all over again when they were being quiescent and gentlemanly. I said "Not bad, all things considered. Not bad at all." *Nugas* took the answer seriously, commenting that the bastinado works wonders with a *recalcitrant* guest, and I wondered where he picked up such an obscure word, maybe from the British? The active, spunky part of me was working hard to dispel all thoughts of further torment. I willed it to stop.

It worked all right. The whole of the next day I spent in restorative foot repair, a mending process due to take weeks, but beginning now with the welts and sores visible, but poulticed and strangely muted, the result of not being battered again. On the whole we said little, though I marveled at his surprisingly-developed English just as if he had been waiting for me all along to brighten his day. I had the distinct feeling after the parlous opening salvo that this was going to be a successful sortie, vastly different from the outset. There was mercy in his very glance at my maltreated heels.

I even permitted myself a cheerful thought or two, quoting to myself Robert Ruark's mot about the Cape buffalo of Africa: "They look at you as if you owe them money." That for starters, and then the *sotie* attributed to Virgil who said to some goddess "ask not me to repeat unspeakable grief" (I the scholar interrupting everything with classic tags). I have the Virgil wrong, it's clear to me, but what can you expect from a man who's just been bastinadoed for half-an-hour? This much, and no more.

Toward mid-afternoon, an unnamed member of the establishment appeared. Again, the cheery greeting, the query about my health, the reassuring pat on my knee to let me know that the dose would not be repeated.

"Your name?" I asked.

"What's in a name?"

"That depends," I answered. "Who are you anyway?"

"That remains to be seen," he said. "How are the feet?"

"They hurt like hell," I reported with unusual force.

"Keep them that way. Now, since you are lively, give me the story of Light Lomax, found wandering among the dunes."

"I was amazed."

He took a long breath, designed to shake him free of some insidious air-monster, and began reciting to me for some reason, the circumstances of capital punishment in Mongolia. "First," he almost crowed as if declaiming something over familiar, "treason, of course, then espionage, political murder, political murder of a representative of a foreign power, premeditated murder, rape with or without bodily assistance, the rape of a minor, the attempted murder of a militia worker or policeman or militia volunteer, and wrecking."

"What," I inquired, stupefied by his long list of malefactions, "is wrecking?"

He answered readily. "It has to do with ships, boats."

"I thought Mongolia didn't have ships," I said, plagued by visions of the Gobi Desert and beyond.

"We have lakes," he said. "And that is enough." I seemed to recall an assault on China way back when, the trouble being with ships, poorly constructed and caught in a storm. So they all drowned, and there was no one left to execute.

"Just so," he said with a jolly expression. "Just so," adding, "the death penalty is not applied to women or men under 18 and aged beyond 60. We are not savages. Execution is by shooting."

"Glad to hear it," I retorted, since in any case it did not concern me.

"The people have a right to appeal within 10 days, to a special court. Again, we are not savages, although we maintain the law."

This insight into the terminal problems of the Mongolese converted me on sight, in spite of my battered heels. It was good to see somebody who knew how to do things on demand. "We didn't get our first President until September, 1990, so clemency petitions were considered by the Presidium of the People's great Hurrah. In the old days executions were more numerous, now down to a dozen a year."

Again, I wondered why so much information was being directed my way. I already knew more than I needed to, and my interlocutor had by no means finished with me. "It all depends on a Special Rapporteur," he said, "who was famous for his likening our political system to that of Georgia or Nepal, which had in common the secret abuse of condemned prisoners, especially those confined in Prison No. 405 (Takhir Soyot)." Those whose lives began and ended in the isolation regime were the most unfortunate of all. "Take the case of Seded Bataa," he said, "who died on July 22, 2005, following his transfer from Zuumod Pretrial Detention Center on July 5. On his arrival, he was bloated, unable to speak. His condition post mortem was TB, but he was neither gaunt nor emaciated. There were bruises and welts around the ankles and wrists consistent with reports of his being continuously handcuffed and shackled in his cell. His personal effects were not returned. His Special Rapporteur claimed that Seded Bata had been tortured to death, which was why his body had not been returned to his family for burial."

"Makes you glad that you are in the hands of Zuumad rather than Tahir Soyot."

Initially unsuspicious, in spite of my heels, I now grew apprehensive. Too much talk of torture, too much talk of death.

"We are getting ahead of ourselves," he said abruptly with a wry twist of his ancient features. "We want to introduce you to the 'flying in space', which consists of a stool's being kicked repeatedly from beneath the recipient of the procedure. This produces the most exquisite *angoisse* as the French call it, the sudden jolt and surprise eventually maiming the legs. It does make a mess, but I'm sure you are conditioned to that. I *am* sorry for the repetitions, but there you have it. Always in the hands of dolts, learning the ins and outs of police techniques."

"But why me? Why am I being subjugated to such awful treatment?"

"Oh, has nobody told you? For having brutalized your companion, Mr. Lomax."

He went on, "sparing you the usual punishments of needles pushed under fingernails, electric shock, burning with cigarettes, prolonged periods of being shackled with handcuffs, constant physical abuse, and the habitual restraints of lawyers and families—the absence of both, in fact. All this you are spared. He said this with some pride, as if proffering me the lap of luxury, and singling out his one *chef d' oeuvre* for extra praise because, well, it was the most recent.

"All for me," I gestured hysterically.

"Oh no, just the flying space. We are nothing if not selective."

"You jest, of course."

"We are deadly serious. You will see."

"When?"

"Minutes away, actually."

This was unlike the behavior of the English of old, tying someone with a rope and dropping him from a hangable height. This was degrading and disgraceful, an abomination of friendship and a vengeful untruth. I wondered where Lomax was and where they had purloined his famous leg.

The rest is silence as the stool was repeatedly withdrawn, and I fell time and again on my battered legs to the amusement of several observers, mainly two, minus *Bodon G*. In fact, it was not amusing at all, but mechanical and bland. Why this ranked so high on their list of torture implements eluded me. The old style would have worked better, if what was wanted was the prisoner being reduced as fast as possible to a howling nitwit. No, this was a novelty (exactly what he had said it was), designed to please.

As time went by, my legs, which had tensed up anticipating each fall, began to grow numb, and my exclamations of torpid horror began to disappear into silence. The two or three watchers left me to it, and eventually the torture machine was switched off.

"Let that be a lesson to you. You have ten days before being executed." Said by a faceless drone out of sight. I slept nonetheless, confident in my rescue by a posse of illustrious lawyers who would be indignant at my treatment and close up the police station for good.

TEN

Imagine the shock I felt when waking to my customary mental diet of UFOs and re-dreaming the events of the phantom apparition that flew through the hospital, daring me to cut it down to size.

Imagine still further the palpable ghost of Lomax, both legs intact, snoring beside me in his usual fashion, not trekking through the Gobi or anywhere else.

Imagine the waking reunion of the two men, the one just finishing a normal sleep, the other saved from the torments of execution. How on earth did they manage to speak to each other? Which they did not, for a full five minutes, one lost in a dream that never happened, the other with ten days to spare before the bullets found their home.

"Slept well?" He.

"Better than usual." I. No need for more, not while adjusting to the new conditions. I wondered if he had any inkling of the last few days—the bastinado. I even dreamed (if such) of the old days: *Nugas, Tarvag, Bodon G.,* and of my taxi driver as he pretended to scour the desert. With such a wealth of lucid dreaming, I would be preoccupied for the rest of my life, afraid that it would all come back to haunt me, while he became used to the extra degree of consideration I planted in my dealings with him.

I dream dated an art of metempsychosis, which I remembered as recovery of a potent reverie of someone invading another's head, and I wondered by what angle he would approach such a transition of souls. He said nothing, but he thought a lot and I could sense his dubiety through the maze of his thoughts. You might say I was closer to him than usual, close in the sense of shared experience, but I never alluded to the time of the gifts, or the cultivation of *Nugas* (Nougat), *Tarvag,* and *Bodon G.*, those mythic people from the Gobi Desert, land of dinosaur skeletons.

I even shrank from asking him if he had been away a couple of times or only once. Let sleeping dogs lie, I told myself, there was no point in disturbing his memories.

Perhaps, when we reached our 80th year, if we ever did. Then would be the time, if ever, to swap experiences, his take on snow and Chernobyl, mine on being pummeled and threatened with execution, the whole thing blurred by times relentless interference. Perhaps there would be no such exchange, but we would improvise imaginary scenes, glad still to be able to instead of descending into our own private Alzheimer's.

We slept better, resumed our dealings with the doxies, and (my initiative) relations with the UFOs, which reappeared to me like the ghosts of Christmas past, just as ambivalent as before but somehow more attuned to the spirit that was surveying them. This is to say they were not any different from what they had been, but were more capable of being looked at, as certain dinosaur skeletons are, replete and august. I find this concept hard to state; let's leave it thoroughly alone for the time being. One of us had aged considerably in the meantime, and I suspected it had not been me, humiliated feet notwithstanding.

After all, as I now belatedly accepted, all the goings-on at the police station had been fodder for the mind, not real at all, but a kind of minatory shadow-boxing, sadistic and officious, but mental the same. Put otherwise, you could say something was different about me, something had changed. I didn't know what. Imagined, they dealt me a formidable blow, but of what I cannot be specific. I retained the memory of being pummeled, that was all, readily transmuted into being a memory of nothing, but *felt* nonetheless.

As you see, I have trouble tying down imaginary happenings which nonetheless leave a mark. I passed easily through the stage of associating this buzz of the system with the UFOs: not their kind of thing at all. But I failed to make it anything else. I had been battered. False. I had not been battered. Really. What was it, then, this feeling of being changed, like a woman negotiating her first or last period, or a man having his first orgasm. Insuperably mental, it sparked a wisp of foreknowledge, with the knees and heels perfectly shaped as before, but with something irretrievably altered, even past death. I presumed the answer would appear, like a puzzle unraveling as I continued to brood on it, giving the devil his increasing due.

The thing was: To what extent did the UFOs feel the change in me? I assumed: No change. But that was facile, and who was I, panjandrum of infinite space, to foist subtle changes on their knowability? Was their response to all of us humans clotting together a touch more severe? Did they automatically downgrade human performance on account of a bastinado threatened but not performed? Surely they had *some* response? Surely not. I left the question to take its own way with the whirligig of ideas, and concentrated instead on Lomax as I should.

What of Lomax, then, back from the dead with legs intact, no after effect from Chernobyl, and deprived of his three henchmen? An earlier version, perhaps? Or one later than thinkable, a complete corpse, if only I recognized it as such. What had he gone through? Had all the events really happened? I doubted it. They had occurred in a mind-blink between lifting a demitasse of espresso from ornate saucer to my chapped lips. I was dealing with a previous Lomax, and therefore more innocent, though with broken legs.

That was my initial impression, one of loyalty, setting aside his injury to come to the aid of a friend in greater need. As *he* thought. I'd rather he had stayed at home, nursing his wounds, but you can't have everything in this world. Then there wouldn't have been the need to find his corpse, no need either to undergo the bastinado or the cult of the flying buttress. This was the heft of all imagination, vastly different from the real, which never left you. I checked myself—both inspired contrasting but legitimate responses—and who preferred which? The ideal, I figured, was to have both, pain and all, to achieve a balanced outlook on what was generally called *life*—provided one knew which was which, if one ever did.

So-called life anyway. I wonder if anybody was capable of saying, "I have lived life to the full," with not a facet missed. Life complete and sated. Life in which the complex oath has been said to the full, as in Ben Kingsley's total abuse of his friend in the movie *Sexy Beast,* a compendium of all the vile things that can be said from one being to another (capped with making water, and missing the toilet completely, on purpose). Or the exhaustive and admirable array of curse words spewed out by one standup comic in a performance so complete it made its appearance as a booklet, dripping with obscenity.

This notion of a partly complete rodomontade, succeeded by another even less complete, gives the lie to our self-deception. Nothing said in full, no matter how long you live, with always an extra blasphemy to come or invented, always a bout of scurrility. This shows blatantly in the list of Aliens, always incomplete which dogs the imagination of even the most thoughtful of us. Who can say he would not like to live any longer? Who can say there is an end, and rest silent thereafter until death? With not a peek at something further? Some few, mostly among the clergy or the pious.

Not me, not Lomax. We added one extra name to the roll-call and so damaged the pretence of totality. Lomax said his little-used French name, *André,* and there was an end to pretending to be complete. I pronounced the word *hiver* (winter) and there stood mine. Always the possibility of saying an extra word ruins the aspiration to exhaustion.

We could have contented ourselves with that superflux until the end of time. After all, something of which he had no memory, and something that haunted me for ever after, in all its brutal nonsensicality, added to my load, which I added to the burden of the Aliens, not knowing where to put it otherwise. Were we waiting for the interregnum of women? Or the last obscenity produced by human hands? Such thoughts, even as incredible as these, dogged my mind until I successfully transferred them to the UFOs.

You see how I haunted myself with things that had happened, that were going to happen, or that never would happen, trying with all my might to keep them apart? I mingled amid the rumpus of shapes, envying Lomax's clearheadedness (thinking he had less to think about) at all levels. And blaming myself for intruding too far into his private processes, which were a mystery to me.

I did it to shed all pretense of 'knowing another', and vowed to wrap myself in my own thoughts, which troubled me no end. I had no knowledge of what happened to him during his departure from my reality, and would not presume to try plumbing it.

He showed no inclination to return to Ithaca, and that was OK by me, except we would soon run out of the drugs that kept us steady, and what then? Both were soft choices: dwindling down to darkness with our last orisons prepared or a flight back to Ithaca with our hearts bleeding out and our lungs failing. We had to calculate such things or die.

And, that said, we returned to duty (What of the world, who's to stay and who depart?), weary of the whole endeavor. He was glad to have survived (he didn't quite know what), whereas I, having had too much, craved an experience humdrum and blank, sufficient to see me through the next few years. I detected in him an accelerated longing for fresh fields and pastures new, understandable in one who remembers naught of dying limbless on the Gobi. I knew he wasn't in a hurry to do it, it just appealed to him as the next thing to do, adumbrated to me in the course of casual conversation, with many a pause while the plan changed or went stale even while being reconsidered.

I remembered something about his being a throttle-jockey for a minor airline (piston engines rather than jet), dismissed as soon as considered, like his longing to join an Arabian power for the excitement of it all. Ditched as soon as considered. I became used to his quicksilver changes, reminding myself what a strident career he already had had, in contrast to myself.

No, he admitted, truth told he had one basic idea left, and that entailed flying to a deserted Japanese island, which had once mined coal, there to build (rebuild) a hotel. One mile distant from the mainland, over which he would fly his kite, swimming the rest of the way if the breeze let him down. He would send for his son later, once the buildings were renewed, of course. He offered me the ground floor, but I demurred, reluctant to spend the rest of my lifetime with coal or hotel. He persisted with the idea nonetheless, gearing up for the experiment with a pair of violet jodhpurs and a lofty hat.

I felt deserted. Having no inclination to move, I didn't find Ulan Bator too bad a place now that the events of the past month began to subside (though my heels still ached, from something half-forgotten). I stuck it out, never dissuading him, but never encouraging him either. Perhaps, after all, he would tire of this madcap idea and come back to earth, if only a return to Ithaca, home and beauty. We still signed ourselves adventurers, of limited experience but boundless ambition, hoping to catch fire again, except in my case not so soon.

Then it started, the avalanche of goodies for the trip, from snowshoes to something he referred to as carbon hammers, from rotund, picturesque air-machines to flashy dry goods implying a world of disguises (I think he planned a different costume every day). He must have had an unlimited supply of money, for he intended to re-erect the whole establishment from the ground up. One thing he had forgotten: entry to this netherworld of carbon and coal was forbidden by the Japanese authorities, so how had he hoped to get past them? He never said, but I suspected bribery, with job offers directed at selected souls intent on being invited for the first Lomax Hotel.

Turning to other matters, I wondered distantly if my tax return had survived scrutiny and if I had my refund. I say distantly, but it was more extreme than that, demanding the use of light-years. By the time I got back, the post office would have upped the rate of a twenty-nine cent letter to 131 cents and beyond, and the accursed Iranians would have seized Palm Beach. The price of everything would have sky rocketed and the bottom would have fallen out of the stock market. The TV would have collapsed into an homage of self-immolation squads and most of the self-styled new reporters would have had their throats cut by a howling mob.

But why should I worry, unlikely to return to the hummingbirds and the forsythia hoard of Ithaca, flowering triumphantly as usual. Civilizations come to the boiling point at differing times, and it is virtually impossible to time one's arrivals as they reach their best, though people have tried, dodging around the world hunting for the best in any given geographic space, such as avoiding Kosovo, Darfur, and Laos in favor of Canada, Dubai, and Switzerland. Call me a hedonist if you like. Then what was I doing in Mongolia? It must have been the lure of the wild that drew me to its bosom, as it did Light Lomax. Or the powerful repute of Genghis Khan himself, who at least twice buried thousands of sailors in a futile effort to annex China.

Something drew me still to the place, in spite of the beatings and Lomax's intended departure. It wasn't the language (God forbid!), but it might have been the climate, cooler than most, the saturnine people, the sparse airline service, the names of the ruins and monasteries that lay scattered about like a head cold that would not go away. Or the promise of things going awry without warning, an anthrax outbreak or a genuine influx of radium (see Chernobyl).

Lomax knocked me out of my reverie with the news that Tabitha with or without his child was on the way to visit and had already reached Ulan Bator to see how things stood in general. For those whose vocation is forgetting, I hasten to add that she was Lomax's house sitter, the one who nursed him. She, to hear him, was a very fine lady with a degree in Mesopotamian literature, who would do us much good at the end of her absurd journey. I couldn't resist asking him what she really wanted, but he knew nothing apart from her willingness to do long journeys for willing partners. I would find out, but she was cutting into my time left with Lomax before he set out for Japan.

The coal mine was dominating Lomax's thoughts, he had softened in his regard for the UFOs, perhaps owing to what he had gone through (if indeed he had gone through it at all). Tabitha did nothing for me, and I thought what a hindrance she would be, ridiculing my UFOs, and changing my mediocre ways. As for the tale of ferrying my pills from Ithaca to Mongolia, I jeered at it. The Post Office would have done the job for me with just one or two queries about forbidden substances. And here she was already in Ulan Bator, lording it over the stewards of flight, just an hour away or less.

All the same, I didn't relish the thought of Lomax fresh back from the dead (or wherever he had been), going absent without leave to a closed old coal mine. I had not even been invited, and I would certainly not have gone. I felt rebuffed. Obsolete even, and it was like the old days with *Nougat, Tarvag,* and *Bodon G.* (who had disappeared, no doubt into the wild boar of himself). I wondered what in truth had become of the whole terrible trio, and had a foreboding that when it was revealed it would be some tale of prismatic horror, with the three no longer in the ascendant.

Asking about her would have pleased Lomax, so I did the contrary, nonetheless imagining her lace-up boots and sullen mien, her drab skirts and horn-rimmed spectacles. Not having any idea of her set me champing at the bit to excoriate.

She would arrive within the hour, unless she did some shopping in Ulan Bator. I wanted to see what she had forgotten and what I would have to buy for myself at one of the clip joints in the city. She was 30-ish, Lomax had told me, and his idea of a "looker", whatever dismal confection that turned out to be. Where would she sleep?

I could not have been more wrong. Raven-haired, she had locks down to her waist, and a tunic of gold down to her feet, which she capped with jet-black high heels. Her voice tootled, "Manolo Blahnik," with an elegant warble and echoed among the rafters of our yurt. She was in all respects vivacious, stylish and high spirited, not the least part of her a woman who should accompany anyone to a coal mine. Nor anyone who belonged in a yurt. She was a classic beauty, she who had left home and glory for a pair of aged adventurers looking for Genghis Khan or one of his team.

Yes, she was worth looking at both aesthetically and with lust, which if memory served me right was to the Ancient Greeks one and the same. She reminded me of the days when I tried to persuade people that literature was the highest aspiration of all—beyond music, say. (Vain hope!) I argued that among the literati there was insufficient homage paid to literature, not enough fidelity, and certainly not enough respect. Arguing against a certain view of literature as no more than workmanlike, I argued both ethereally and practically, for a wider aspect to literary studies and for a more tender, reverential approach to the text. In one mood I argued for the life blood of a master spirit, in another for its being a tough nut to crack.

I soon lost the tough nut to crack (many people read literature in a hurry), but I developed the ethereal as a worthwhile concept, persuading people to take their time, to read a passage several times over before making up their minds, and to develop a habit of seeing literature in the round, not as skimming a set text but as something inexhaustible.

Tabitha reminded me of those days. Her reading of literature was vast, her sympathy huge. We read in the evenings before Lomax's departure, which seemed ever more distant, as if he too found Tabitha irresistible, too much so to be hastened away from. She had with her some Euripides, Barbusse, and Beckett, over which we pored, seeking the *mot juste* in everything (especially Beckett). Never have I done so much close reading as then, going back rather than forward, as if the name of the game were to stay harnessed to the same word for ever and ever, so exquisite and profound it was.

Lomax joined in of course, but arising all the time to check on the weather, the coffee (which she had brought), and the sky. Always suspecting in his imagination of betraying a certain coal mine before he got to grapple with it.

The day dawned. I did not read at all, amazed at the false starts of his mood: "Well, I'll be going now," followed by his tap on the door a minute later, and his lame "Forgotten something." By the time of his final departure, I could take the suspense no more and actually wished he would go, if only down the road apiece.

Finally, he was gone, but we couldn't settle. She lamented the occasion of a middle-aged man's obsession with a defunct coal mine. I regretted his passion for Japan after his episode with Chernobyl.

The Invisible Riviera

Watching him depart with all his worldly goods about him, by taxi this time, I could not suppress a tear although Tabitha seemed, with all her chores of delivery done, somewhat case-hardened, no doubt having said goodbye numerous times. After all, no one else had seen him post his Chernobyl experience and mourned him as well as suffering the bastinado as his proxy. No wonder I cried, not yet thoroughly accepting him as live or dead. He was gone, an abrupt wave which could also have been a welcome to his Japanese home. We shut the door on him and left him to his fate.

It was not hospitable to think of him in his transit of the mile long bridge of sighs before landing safely at the coal mine. He was confident in his ability to navigate the waters, but I was less so. What if his kite or glider failed and he committed *sea-fall* (as it had been described to me one time by a pilot). I cared about the heroism of the man, but I did not trust it through and through. Why he had decided not to sail to his Shangri-la, I could not fathom. Some last blink of glory, perhaps? Some feat of ultimate audacity? He had no audience for it, no Japanese crowd left over from the war. Just himself, as usual, and the extinct coal mine.

Tabitha and I dropped the subject. There was a limit to all that could be said about him and his exploits. We spent the remainder of the day playing chess (at which she was a whiz), beating me time and again in short games until I gave up, suggesting instead a simpler game of snap or snakes and ladders. She was to the manor born for games of any description, and I at long last quit as she soared on to prismatic heights of facile victory, leaving me in the lurch and already wishing I had joined Lomax in his Japanese sortie.

"A charming man though a little introverted." She was bringing the conversation around to Lomax, by now safely out of earshot.

"When you get to know him," I answered in puckish form, "you will realize his thoughts are truly with the UFOs."

"Who?"

"The Unidentified Flying Objects."

"Oh, *those*. I thought they were old hat, long since sent packing."

I had run into another nonbeliever, so I set out to convert her to the company of Aliens, long since abandoned in the lunatic press of events. I regaled her with talk of my solitary experience: the buff color, the opaque windows, the silence of the thing as it hovered for at least fifteen minutes while I trod water, anxious that it might go away. When it did, with a maneuver no aircraft could simulate, it was airborne in an isometric flash.

"With not a single sound?"

"Not one. It was huge, with at least a dozen windows, exposing its flanks, as it were."

"You must have taken an awful lot of ribbing."

"No fear. I told hardly anyone about it."

"Lucky you. No repeats?"

"None, more's the pity. I like your shoes, by the way."

"So you said. Good old Manolo. It's summer after all. Harder job in winter. Getting used to walking in them."

"If ever."

"Oh, you ultimately get the hang of it. Or you quit until it's summer again."

Since we were on such good terms, I confided to her my thoughts about the Aliens, about their silence and the reasons for it, hoping to bring out her playful side. She appeared devoid of what I chose to call reminiscent melancholy, and I was overjoyed. Then it struck me. We were having a conversation in the depths of Mongolia, about Manolo Blahnik shoes, which was good going for anybody, although she seemed to veer away from the very concept of the silent UFOs. Not rich enough for her, not outrageous enough, whereas I found it almost beyond language itself. "Think of it," I exclaimed, "all the thousands of UFOs, and not a sound from any of them. It makes you more than wonder."

"Quite so," she agreed. "But I wouldn't worry about it. It'll all come out in the wash, mark my words." That summed up the subject for her.

All the same, I produced for her during the casual depths of our conversations, an occasional reference to the UFOs, hoping to tempt her back, but to no purpose. And that is how I came to dub her the agent of Manolo Blahnik, a shoe designer born in the Canary Islands (as she explained), Czech heritage, who was soon dressing his pet dogs and monkeys in the styles to which the world would become accustomed. Out of muslin and pink cotton ribbons, he said. One dog would always lie on its back, sticking its paws in the air, while he tied the bows.

"Thus began," she said, "the career of his footwear, in London in Feather's Boutique, and he studied at the Universities of Geneva and Paris. Even with twelve-inch heels," (she flashed both feet to show me), "I feel quite comfortable."

I gaped, not being accustomed to seminars about the intricacies of shoe design from a recent immigrant (or whatever) to Mongolia. How to express it, I don't quite know, but I had already formed a link between Manolo Blahnik and the Aliens, thinking them both creatures of mystery, patrons of absurdity.

Or, one mystery led to the other, without overlapping. Somehow his shoes led to their silence. His outrageous, fawning concepts led to total nothing. As if the ladies lucky enough to wear his gear had reduced themselves to muteness lest they topple off their mounts. Ah, that was it! Now the ladies and the Aliens were at level pegging, sharing the same code of silence. The world was making sense after all, and for the moment I let the matter rest. The bizarre truth would follow in a few days, when my captive soul had settled down and the real mettle of Tabitha had declared itself.

What a joy to repose behind my big idea and talk of other matters. I felt for the first time stripped of my obsession, and with it the perhaps related idea of the bastinado, the threat of execution, the disappearance of Lomax followed by his return. And the hospital shadow factory, ringing the changes on phantom photons, sometimes assuming the shape of airplanes (two-dimensional), sometimes assuming no shape at all other than abrupt shifts in direction. All this and more, amounting to a hectic interior life that had to be calmed down before doing me in.

I felt myself running down, an excursion into one tenth rat power beginning, and I was glad of it.

ELEVEN

The Invisible Riviera

With herself parked next door (thus upping the price I had to pay the Mongolian landlord), I felt somehow balanced as I had never felt with Lomax sleeping next to me. It must have been the unsettling effect of his long legs, the mythical story of which has now been told. The result was that I had an uninterrupted sleep and woke feeling refreshed beyond the norm. Maybe it was her parting shot (after chess and Manolo Blahnik). She said, quoting Madonna (hardly a favorite of mine), something to the effect that Manolo Blahniks were better than sex, adding that, "they last longer." Whether she meant sexual power or resilience (or something akin) or the power of the shoes, I did not quite understand.

Perhaps, being Madonna (of the French tastes), both. And whether Tabitha intended the remark as a come-on to me, I didn't find out until later, as I got to know her and appreciate her even more. She and Madonna were fighting back against the cult of the sensible shoe, and in this they had my full support.

Perhaps there was a sudden feeling that I had on my side three redoubtable personalities, Tabitha, Manolo and to a lesser extent Madonna. That was the source of my newfound balance. Or was it some reinforcement of my feelings about the Aliens, and their vivid manifestation to me of some years ago, confirming my status as a believer: If women felt at ease in 11- or 12-inch shoes, than anything was possible. So said my male chauvinist pig, bitterly aware that male taste in shoes was humdrum and tame. I had not made the leap myself, and that is what the silence of the Aliens was waiting for. I could be the first man to adopt the 12-inch heel, and hark what crescendo followed, a heavenly chorus of plangent cheers that lasted for days.

I calmed down after breakfast with Tabitha, drawing myself back from my tendency to whoopee everything in sight, especially with Lomax gone. Tabitha consumed coffee like a Turk, no doubt clothing her naked body first in coffee, then in the 12-inch Manolo of the day.

Came the cheese, *byaslag,* an inelegant name for a costive substance, and the jam (*jimsnii chanamal*), which had a pepperminty-orange flavor. We soon got by this unprecedented bouquet of horrors and resumed our conversation about Manolo Blahniks, about which Carrie Bradshaw, of *Sex and the City* fame, told a mugger: "You can take my Fendi baguette, my ring and my watch, but *don't* take my Manolo Blahniks." He did as he was told. We cheered for Carrie Bradshaw, sticking to her guns.

After that, we went out to see the sights, which Tabitha took in with bemused ecstasy, viewing everything for the first time—the police station (of recent pain), the infirmary, the old man with wizened teeth who ran the taxi, the cheese store, and the airport road (which she had seen before), and such-like beauties. After which I said, "You'll be pining for home after all this Mongoliata."

"No way. It has an insipid color."

"Honestly?"

"Think of Lomax, buried in coal," she answered.

I didn't envy him.

It was fun getting to know her amid all her Manolo Blahnik exuberance, much different from Lomax, although they had in common their dislike of UFOs. I was living in a fool's paradise, since she was scheduled soon to depart, back to the verdant paradise of springtime Ithaca. When I asked about this, she begged off the question, saying what was my hurry? Was I also impatient to get back to my own home, handily rented to a house sitter, an expert in Russian literature and a budding novelist? Not a bit of it, I protested. Let him get on with his novel. "I've already done enough of that kind of thing. For now."

She let the notion drop, instead began trying to learn the difficult language of the Mongol people, and became strangely preoccupied with my own heels, which had not forgotten the bastinado, as I called it. It would be a long time before they healed completely and I returned to Ithaca a whole man.

She devoted much of her time to asking about Lomax, whom she knew little and found picturesque. She had noticed his peculiar habits during the short stay in his house, such as his liking for checkerboard patterns of Chinese manufacture, his disinclination to give his son, Noah, anything that did not please him first (no wife in attendance), his longing to be out in the world, sampling its most outrageous aspects (Chernobyl, the distant coal mine in Japan), and his passion to repair things, which he did with uncanny skill and high prices. He liked camping out (his son did not), and had a genuine fondness for winter, which his son abominated. The son, she observed, was "a bright little bugger" of nine years, home-schooled except for the long intervals when Lomax was away, and Noah was left to the wiles of successive nannies, of whom she was the most recent. Her husband, rarely mentioned, although asked about, dealt with cooking and pleas for help from those unlucky souls seeking a geek, because they had been saddled with expensive audiovisual equipment they could not understand.

All in all, thanks to an observant and inquisitive nature, she knew him pretty well considering her short stay in the *ménage,* and sued to know him better despite the hopeless gravitations of his wanderlust. She asked and I responded, omitting all talk of his hospital stay and my being threatened with execution. You can have too much of a good thing, even at the hands of a woman who wears the exquisite vertical filigree of Manolo Blahnik.

The Invisible Riviera

When she finally left, I would be alone again, with a surfeit of pills and coffee. Fresh meat for the depredations of the Mongols, whose jaunts with me were surely not complete. Perhaps, this time, they would spirit me away for a hurried execution, an even more hurried funeral. Where had *Nougat, Tarvag,* and *Bodon G.* gone while I was preoccupied with Lomax's departure and Tabitha's arrival? I had the sense people were waiting me out, just to have at me again, this time no holds barred.

Had I known more, I would have been less happy. Lomax was already on his way across the mile strait to the deserted mine, winging his way to glory, with an evil wind buffeting him about, and sudden downdrafts making him lose one hundred feet of his five hundred gained. In my mind's eye, I watched him land safely, but untidily short of towers that dwarfed him, right at the water's edge, and it excited him to be hemmed in on his arrival between deep water and monoliths. He made it after all, and scrambled, fumbling, up the incline to the steep side.

Going from her cockahoop splendors to mentally reviewing his risky doings was no picnic, plummeting to his death down deep chimneys. Life with Lomax had its joys, life without him had turned into a maze of grim guesswork.

I did not blame him for this, but I began to guess which ordeal he would face next, the Black Hole of Calcutta, for which he had to go to Calcutta (natch), or a Black Hole of astronomy, brocaded in such pleasant terms as *singularity* or the *event horizon*. Nothing could escape either. They would at least dispatch him from my ken, whereas something from the other blackness would leave pieces of him dangling, to be sported about with. You could see which side of blackness I was on. A trip through a lighthearted landscape won me over every time, especially when you considered the hell I had been through.

The more I thought of him, ensconced in left-behind miner's lamps, the more I wished he had stayed with us to inspect the zany world of spindly, unwearable shoes. If you are going to make a botch of your life after living most of it with civilized decorum, you should enjoy it, not consign it to Blackness of one kind or other, waiting for the absolute event horizon to strip you down in a flash to stretched out linguini, from which there is no return.

Thus my revised new syllabus of how to prosper in life. Find something preposterous and sink your very being into it full scale, and who cares if the result is a shoe nobody can wear. You have given your all, and that is what counts, while waiting for the Aliens to spring to vocal life, as the world goes downhill to darkness.

I had many such thoughts, most of them despondent, the only bright patch when I thought of returning, as an opossum or nuthatch, in several million years to see what a mess the Aliens had made of "our" world in the meantime.

"You're silent today," she said. "Been brooding about Lomax?"

"He and others," I replied.

"He's a big boy, capable of making his own decisions."

"Not as capable as you, madam."

"The devil's gateway," she tooted, "is always open."

She was quoting something or other. You could tell it by the modular tone of the utterance, a bit higher than usual, even a little falsetto.

"I was just wondering how he was faring among the natives," I said. "Looking out for him."

"I wouldn't myself. Always take men as you find them. It's easier that way."

We stopped off at a lunch counter for a slice of barley bread, and then resumed our *chauferesca*. She, it seemed, was stocking me up for two seasons, the imminent summer and the succeeding fall (if I stayed that long). First, a round of sweets, from honey to mints, from glazed nuts to Dolly Mixtures (shades of my not exactly abandoned childhood of long ago). We took two taxis, and I wondered how such confectionary made its appearance in such an out-of-the-way place as Ulan Bator.

Then we turned our attention to prosaic things, local musk aftershave, and Kiehl's Centella Recovery Skin-Salve Clinically Demonstrated to Soothe Temporarily Irritated and Sensitive Skin. A title so long could hardly err in bringing relief from whatever ailed you. Plus Estánd de Oro Proteccion (A & D) and a gel for mouth eruptions. By which point I lost count, seeing that half our purchases were in a foreign tongue I had neither the inclination nor time to ferret out. Taxi number three followed this excursion, and the collection of bags grew, to be supplemented by bigger and more expensive bags with classier logos.

How on earth did the Mongolian stores, such as they were, come to stock such stuff? Only for visitors, like the Gum stores in Communist Russia. I would never again lack for sweetmeats or lotions, whatever tricks fate played on me next.

Then we moved on to her requirements, which amounted to small bags of chocolate goodies the names of which I hardly knew to ornamental boxes of potions and trinkets I only guessed at, from decorated shoehorns to assorted boxes from which emerged surreptitious odors of patchouli, jasmine, and mountain heather. Clearly she was getting ready to leave me to it, marooned in friendless isolation near the Gobi Desert, and not so long since she'd arrived. I accepted my punishment without complaint, however, and inquired as to her next port of call.

"Why, back to Ithaca, of course. Where my husband is waiting for me."

Some husband, I murmured, as our quotient of bags increased and my feelings developed into smarts. Everyone had someone to return to, husband or offspring, except Lomax and me, and he had a son to hear the interminable tales of Mongolia, Chernobyl, and the Japanese coal mine.

"Leaving when?" was my surly response. "Tomorrow?"

"Hardly. We haven't even skimmed the barrel." She clearly intended to do more shopping, her final taxi loaded to the gills with stuff that surely cost her a fortune in local currency.

Hours later, we unloaded our booty and, laughing, relaxed on the bed in my quarters.

The next thing amazed me. She offered me the deed of kind, full access to her body, which I, for all my fatigue, accepted, puffing away for what seemed hours with my assignment. She did it out of kindness, for helping with all that shopping, but I wish she hadn't. I saved myself up for such occasions, and I was hardly in fit shape to conduct *amours*, still less with someone due to flit away on the next jet.

A mood of profound disinclination swept over me as, in my imagination, I grilled her about the circumstances of her intended departure. As in: "Who are you going to miss most?" Unanswered, mainly because of my barbarous tone, but also, I reasoned, not to give offence.

Then: "Whom have you missed most while away on your mercy mission, delivering essentials, pills and such?" Nothing but the same quizzical smile.

After which: "Did you enjoy our being together?" A shrug was my answer, meaning don't boast about it.

Then I tried, on a different track: "Does Noah miss his father?" She shrugged an answer. (Of course.) "But," she added, "he's not much of a cry baby, anyway. He gets by. He's used to it."

I tried further. "How do you fly?"

"First," came the answer, quick as thunder. "When I can."

And on I went, interrogating her. The simpler my questions grew, the more she cooperated, but I knew the questions which would provoke no answer. About sex, she was mum. Her mind must have been far away, on Lomax, with whom she had probably slept, but when? We had all been so close until he left.

Perhaps she found his departure too abrupt. Did she miss her husband? Only tangentially. She was at her happiest while shopping, even in such a pestilential hole as Ulan Bator. What was her plan? To be home, where the heart traditionally spends all its summers, with hubby and someone else's child.

We were running out of conversation, and I resisted all talk of the bastinado; eerie moments of discovery flanked by other moments of blank apprehension; the long hours in the hospital, the mystifying shape that hovered in my imagination, took off and landed, returning to the same point of departure like an airplane restricted to only two dimensions.

All this denied, which is to say *denied her*, who was the soul of giving in many ways. To tell the truth, I would have told her more if I had only believed myself capable of making sense of it all. Such as the horny hand of my eighty-year-old taxi driver. She would get over it (never having known it), I told myself.

One kiss of farewell, a peck on the cheek equivalent to a peck on the teeth, and she was gone in a taxi crowded with her shopping. I felt again the pangs of manufactured loneliness, but had only myself to blame. Besides, I also felt relief now that everyone had gone, and I was once more alone with my toys.

There was nothing to do but wait for the first letter from Lomax, full of excitations self-induced. But no letter came and I had to resort to the local library to confirm where he had gone and that he was not whiling his time away in Hawaii.

Hashima Island was a ragged slab of concrete that once had been a thriving mine, with a population density unparalleled on earth. Some fifteen miles off Nagasaki, the treeless settlement was distinguished, for a time, by high-rise Manhattan-style peaks, jostling against the seawall.

He had told me this before departing, combining the tones of someone whose face took in both ecstasy and dread. How could his face express both? By assigning different feelings to different parts? This gave him an odd look, the rictus of the professional traveler, half looking backward to home and glory, the other half meeting perils with a stout face, determined to prevail. I had not seen him like this, ever, and the sight of him abominably perplexed made me want to join him in what could be the last of his madcap enterprises. After that, only quiet chats with his son by the hearth and the festooning sickness of travel tales, put in their proper place among the eccentricities of Grandad Lomax.

I found *this* Lomax easier to stare down. His quirk of an unblinking level gaze usually quailed, as if from something shameful or stupendously awful. This was not the face of a man who had been to Chernobyl and come back, presumably immune to its horrors. Of his courage, there was no doubt, but some would have said his duty was to be with his son, and, not like the fighter pilots of the old days, doom-laden, off to massacre the Hun as the first store of business. Still, he had something of the fighter pilot braggadocio, silk scarf and Bryl-cremed hair, but marred by the habit of scrutinizing things too closely and too unyieldingly.

He could still be jolly, oh yes, but with a downward cast, as if he expected half his face to be shot away or burned beyond recognition, as happened to so many of the "First of the Few." Perhaps he was afraid of contaminating his son with such an outcome, sufficient to extort looks of barren pity from women who would have sufficed to bear him a child. I had not heard of this particular war injury, but I could believe in it, for I was the proud bearer of my father's war scar, I possessed the precise blemish of his own, a twinned serenade of pink flesh for both of us. There must be a word for such an event, cicatrice or something like, and I vowed to look it up.

I remembered something Lomax had told me of Hashima's long descending tunnels, seams of coal below the actual ocean, and how they disgorged enormous burdens of black fuel for almost a century. Who could resist that? Not Lomax, at any rate. But in 1974 the miners abandoned it all as played out and headed for the mainland, leaving behind headgear, miner's hats, fragments of explosives. As he'd said, only a few cats and dogs remained to populate the island.

To be so decisive was an enviable trait. At least I found it so, contrasted with my own lackadaisical habits. How different we were, he the prince of souls, and me the man obsessed with the silence of the UFOs. An interesting blend of personalities to say the least, a personable mix of the heroic and the ethereal, both in search of a substance, vanished coal and vanished voices, both doomed to glorious failure. The question is why?

As soon as answered, ignored. I am not in the habit of being sphinxed by interrogatives as bold as that. Why am I alive at all? Why must I die? These unanswerables waited their turn in the shallow valley of discarded things.

To fill the void, I tallied up my theories about the Aliens.

> 1. They keep silent because human brutality sickens them, and they wait for peace.
> 2. They are all set to take over once we have exterminated ourselves.
> 3. They keep silent because we are essentially spouting baby talk.
> 4. They have bypassed language, do not need it, having advanced so far beyond us.
> 5. None of the UFOs are real, not yet anyway. Their response is hidden among the stars, and will be so until they start recording us at our fearsome play.

6. Their first word will be so profound and unsurpassable that we humans will lapse into a painful and permanent silence of our own. This I refer to as the Alien takeover.
7. Perhaps deriving from (6): they do not speak ever, theirs is not a vocal means of communication, and who knows what prodigies of mind-lingo occur in their gleaming chariots?
8. We have not *seen* a single Alien, and who knows what that life form will amount to when we do. A nation of hyperactive frogs? A nation of plasmoids amounting to birds? A crew that speaks with one voice, unrecognizable to us? A valley of loud elephantiasis, braying and trumpeting their triumph?

Once you started this game, you could go on until the end of time. Musing thus, in the renewed absences of Lomax and Tabitha, coal and snow as I dubbed them, I reached delicious rapture, a serenade of blankness, a point at which I discovered the domain of silence at last. There was no need for all that verbiage, centuries long, in which the world quarreled; and hope, disguised as vital promise, died a helpless death. At that point I went to sleep, my form of nothing else to do.

This was (not for the first time) to dream of Ur-horses, those frisky, diminutive occupants of the steppes, not my ideal conveyance by any means, but makeshift rides. The horses that I rode in dreamland were always stationary. In particular, one with piebald mane and flame-colored forelock attracted my eye again and again, perhaps the mount of Genghis Khan himself (excluding his disastrous performances on the high seas). This was the horse I "rode" shamefacedly facing backward. Then I dreamed more serious things, such as the bastinado of recent acquaintance and the Lomax who had come back from the dead to take up coal mining.

Dreams I call them, but they were mainly horrors, even the horse that I rode backwards. Was there a point, I wondered, at which we started dreaming of horrors to come in the wen of history? Had I reached it at last?

To dream of the future entailed shocking myself to death. Life would not be worth living, not even when enlivened by such presences as those of Lomax and Tabitha. I rummaged around in my head for something to make life worth enduring, and found only absent friends, and the idea of visiting them seemed to vitiate their ongoing private capers. I held on bravely, as I thought I had the distinct sensation of having come to the end of it all, and readied myself for the instant of not waking.

Which transformed itself into blissful, neutral sleep, an hour at most, but sufficient to bring me back to semi-normal in which I pillaged breakfast before having even thought about it. Back to the old treadmill of thought, I decided, the endless speculation as to what they were doing now, Lomax and Tabitha, what scrapes they were getting into, with what stupendous results. This got me through until I realized it would see me no further, so I shifted to *whats*. Namely, what did Lomax discover at the bottom of the mineshaft, and how would Noah respond to news of his father a hundred feet down?

It was possible, I thought, to live entirely in imagination, if only one kept imagination at full tilt, none of your makeshift categories but only fresh-minted discoveries of vintage material. Fond hope. I kept obsessing about the same things, tossing the whirligig of thought only to find it repeating. OK. I was obsessive, so I made love to obsession by expanding until I had Lomax perpending over the same fragment of coal, again and again, deeper each time, and Tabitha concentrating on a little boy's flushed cheeks until they occupied the whole universe.

This worked rather well, as long as I made room for it, pushing hard so as not to think of something else. I tried intervening myself into the morass of it, but that did not work, and then imagining Tabitha as Lomax and vice-versa, but that didn't work either. Too much mess, so I went back to my old ritual amplification, getting better at it bit by bit until my exaggerations met one another in mid-stream and I began to interfere with them all over again.

It will come as no surprise to you that, confronted by such barren chances, I decided to say goodbye to the Mongols, gathering my worldly possessions into a heap (pills, my battered copy of *Gulliver's Travels*, maps and summer outfits), and set out for Japan, truly not that far away. Why I had let him go there in the first place, I could not remember, but it was a foolhardy choice. I glimpsed my successor peering down the room as I left it, the same ne'er-do-well as had burdened my taxi. Clearly going up in the world, thanks to the money I had lavished upon him.

Myself, I had plenty of money, brought along as if I meant never to return. Now here I was again, committing myself to another wild goose chase in pursuit of my friend. Come the day (soon) when I tired of this dreadful habit and set up shop in the wilds of Ithaca, to wait my turn at the tumbril.

Suffice to say, I reread *Gulliver's Travels* en route for easily the fourth or fifth time (marveling at the horses), and noting how good-natured a book it was. Swift, however, was a sarcastic man, cutting and vexatious. I would not have liked him, but I liked his book.

Japanese airlines have that little simpering attitude to you. They smile back at you even when you return their gaze with stony impunity, as if committed forever to the same sentimental grimace. I fancied the real expression was one of oblique hatred, waiting for the ax to fall on yet another American goon. I too remembered, without having been there, the Bridge on the River Kwai, falsely named or not, and the Death March of some of my junior friends. In no time we were flying over the Mongol Plateau, some place (I inquired) called Hohhot, which sounded like a hesitant monk swearing.

I was headed for the quiet life among the defunct mines, where Lomax and I could while our time away, singing to one another Chinese and Japanese songs in memory of the thousands of miners who had quitted Hashima Island. The seascape with not a single tree (Lomax had warned me, so I presumed he had known all along that I would go after him). Only the cats survived, he said, so we were guaranteed peace broken only by the sounds of purring.

Alert to my fate, in my absent-minded sort of way, I transacted with an English-speaking Japanese to ferry me across to Hashima, first having amassed an amazing quantity of tinned food and bottled water. Just in case. I did not know how provident Lomax was, maybe losing his sense of practicality in the excitement of the journey. Insisting that the boatman return in a week, to, as I presumed, bring selves off the island or replenish our supplies, we set off for a bumpy ride, with not a trace of coal or cinders in the air, but the air full of a fierce spray that made us dodge as we made our choppy way.

I should have spent the time noticing the spray or the chop, but (such is the mind's aberrant way) spent it plunging down to the days when the mine was full of pitmen, making the long descent to the regime of the coal beds near the ocean bottom. There they were, covered with coal dust, sweating and gasping and chipping away at the exposed coal surface with picks until the seams gave out or the holes they dug became too deep. In 1869, the imported mining engineers from Scotland discovered a seam far underground, and the Takashima started in full production. That was at a depth of some forty-five meters.

To shrug at this was normal, seeing it was ancient history. But I swear it was imagining the noise of the pick-axes chipping away that drew me down to them, the miners risking life and limb for one Thomas B. Glover, scion of a mining family. This coal was better than Welsh, much better than North Country, as it generated less ashes, clinker and soot. I took this information from Lomax. Before he left, he could think of nothing else but coal, its history and provenance, at whose demise he had been willing to assist. He was going to do it all alone, yet here I was, in fitting symmetry traveling to help him.

Finally, the impatient sea abated and I climbed the rocky ascent that used to be a platform. No one to meet me, of course. I had no idea of where Lomax was, and resigned myself to seeking him out. My belongings followed me, inspired by a Japanese shove, and I was alone again. The boat sped away, as if glad to be rid of me, another coal-breather, and I got my first local scent, sweetish, which might not have been the real thing at all, but what else was there on the island to smell of? Looking back, I recognized it as the odor of naptha surviving long past its best.

Five workers a month had died in pit accidents and were cremated on Nakanoshima, a minor island serving Hashima, and I wondered if Lomax had made the side trip to see the site and the furnace which burned their remains. The miners had lived on bean dregs and boiled rice with sardines, which together formed an aromatic, salty paste. The workers suffered much from diarrhea, but were exhorted to keep working by hardnosed guards. And several actually drowned themselves, trying to swim to freedom, *anything* to quit what was also known as "Battleship Island."

I imagined a population of five thousand, jammed into a space that included a primary school, a junior high, gymnasium and pinball parlor, a movie theater, bars, twenty-five retail stores, a hospital, hairdresser, Buddhist temple, Shinto shrine and even a brothel where sooty hands clutched at basic nirvana. No cars, though. All were accommodated in interconnected labyrinthine corridors, which served as the island's private subway system. This was Mitsubishi's island, devoid of the slightest soil.

It is hard to think back to the old impenitent ways in which a hierarchy reigned supreme, with unmarried miners interned in one-room apartments, married Mitsubishi workers and their dependents in six-mat rooms (with shared lavatories, kitchens, and bathrooms) and, most exalted of all in two-bedroom apartments with kitchen and flush toilets. The manager of Mitsubishi Hashima Coal Mine occupied the only private wood-constructed quarters on the island, a house located symbolically at the summit of Hashima's rock face.

Mitsubishi owned the island and everything on it, exercising a benevolent dictatorship that insisted on free housing, electricity and water in return for house cleaning and maintenance of all public facilities. The people huddled together in this bee-worker fascism for as long as they could stand it, and longer indeed, subscribing to "The Company" and all that went with it, attached against their wills (as time went on) to a common purpose leading to a mythical heaven for those who survived. The fresh water had to be carried to the island (until the arrival in 1957 of freshwater pipes connecting to island reservoirs). Sea storms, until then, that prevented the docking of ships for more than a day, were a continued threat to the island's wellbeing and the safety and comfort of all inhabitants.

Few of them had time to take stock of the island, although a movie was shot in 1949 (a postwar thing full of peace and postwar piety), aptly named *Midori Naka* (*The Greenless Island*). The director rapidly appraised Hashima as a rim of coal slag embedded around a bare rock, nothing more, nothing less. Hardly a thing to contemplate for long or to extol as a miracle of housing. Here, until the coal gave out, they lived and died. In 1903, Lomax told me, fresh from immersion in the island's lore, the residents were allowed to use soil imported from the mainland to make rooftop gardens for vegetables and flowers. Electric rice cookers soon followed, and many thought they had gone to heaven. When the inevitable refrigerators and television sets arrived, the thinking people of the island decided it was not heaven after all, but what they had a right to from the very beginning.

The crash came (1960), when petroleum replaced coal and the country's coal mines began to close, with successive contingents of Hashima workers being sent elsewhere, heedless of promises. The end followed in 1974 with a ceremony in the island gymnasium, when the mine was officially closed and the exodus (those who had survived previous purges) began. When the last ship bound for Nagasaki boarded on April 20, 1974, the final resident stepped on, holding an umbrella up to light rain, which the passengers saw as a token of mournful serendipity. He glanced briefly at the deserted apartment blocks which had formerly promised a lifetime of back-breaking toil, stepped on board, and was engulfed in the ship engine's final blast. Enter Lomax, years later.

TWELVE

When I arrived, I found hopeful seagulls prospecting for the scraps of long ago. You would have thought they knew better than to waste time fishing for nonexistent life (unless they intended to plunder Lomax's body down to the last sinew). This is what happens to a country that exhausts its own resources and makes a fetish of outside trade. Dead, desolate, ignored (apart from Lomax's presence somewhere on the island), Hashima spoke to my condition as the last of its kind, a dump awaiting resurrection as a playground for millionaires who never arrived.

During its career as a thriving metropolis, it produced some 16.6 million tons of coal, like a huge battleship at anchor, static and forgotten, wasting away bit by bit until the crack of doom. This had been my first impression as it loomed in the distance, rather statuesque and regal, eventually shedding its battleship quality for a different image, that of an abandoned Alcatraz.

I perched on the dock, little knowing what to do next, with my rudimentary possessions grouped around me, hardly enough to make a grown man puff carrying them uphill. The smell of naptha came and went, dissolved in the coarse cries of the disappointed seagulls, and I began to cry, having sentenced myself to such a ghostly place, with no idea where Lomax was. Who was I to spurn the delights of Mongolia, not to mention China, for this palace of spring clouds and barnacle-clad shabby concrete installations, for all the world like a massive schooner that had lost itself, just preparing to lower the gangplank for the passengers to disembark. The devastation spoke to me in negatives, all the lost glory that might have been. Useless now, it had an air of massive tedium, some bottomless pit of woe wherein all went down the mine—its workers, the rocky island itself—down to the ravenous fishes and the deep sea trench.

At last I pulled myself up and began to explore in a diffident way that spelled out my lack of genuine interest. I hoped to wake up and find myself ensconced in a snowy egret's nest, somewhere cozy and comfortable. All the windows were broken, the first things to go (I wondered: *Why?*). Some sense of completion, perhaps, some inclination for closure? Glass crunched underfoot everywhere I walked. Immense stretches of plaster had fallen from the walls. Sundered shutters creaked in the fierce wind and clattered their own celibate symphony.

The farther I strolled, the more debris piled up: defunct electrical appliances; rotten furniture including some specimens at least fifty years old and black with mold; a barber's shop with rusty scissors still on show; chair covers shriveled; on the walls movie posters of forgotten films dating back to silent days. On one wall I noticed the hours of sailing for the ferry to Nagasaki, clock and calendar for voyages of relief that wouldn't arrive, lost in the straits of never-was.

When I dashed into a building to seek refuge from the rain, the chaos resumed. I headed for the top floor, thinking falsely that the higher up you went the gentler would be the impact of falling roofs, and finally found a section of not quite obliterated roof to shelter under and rest. In general, the building looked like the survivor of an earthquake or a tsunami. What had not crashed down had crashed up again from the impact of so many floors.

But, as I say, I found a niche to roost in, a partly disintegrated ruin held together by an angle in the structure. I noticed a piece of plastic which an earlier visitor had bound around the head of a Buddha, which in some distant, disheveled way evoked a bandaged soldier, fresh from the fray. Unfortunately, the bandage had slipped, tricking the face into an effigy of Saddam Hussein, hanged with appropriate damage to the finer structures of the neck. Or maybe the cheated occupants, deprived of home and work, had hanged the statue of Buddha, leaving him there, a nominal Bantu, to remind the occasional visitor (if any) of the dire misfortunes that could afflict any cruising optimist.

I now realize I lardered together an unnamed soldier, Buddha, and the Bantu, but this is the way my opportunistic mind was working, flitting from one identifiable object to another when all was devastated and unidentified. Revenge personified. Was it mindless vandalism to treat the mini-city in this way, as a last indignity before hopping on to the final boat, or an inevitable consequence of nature, because a thing left to its own devices was bound to fall down? I sided with the vandals who stomped their fury into the corridors and rooms, destroying the windows one by one, ripping up *tatami* mats, and especially the gilded door to the manager's. This kind of frenzy had a right to be. After all, they were going to an unknown future from a hell based on coal. No future at all. No wonder they made hay in the terrible solitude of their adopted city, with not even cockroaches to crush, or pallid flowers to stamp out amid the disintegrating concrete.

Then I found it, a spray painted, half-erased sign, which according to my hasty new minted Japanese vocabulary read ROT. I too, immersed in this time battered city, felt reckless anger, being alone among the ruins. But at least the rain had stopped, and I wandered outside again, having secreted my pitiful possessions in a corner of an extinct room that offered most of itself to the sky.

Three layers confronted me. The shambling, torn-up coal. The bland, blank of the plasterboard, ten feet at least. And the deserted void out of which grew the dilapidated windowless buildings, some with mansard roofs. It was an anonymous contribution to an architecture unremembered to this day, a Maginot Line of Ciphers thrown aside by a coal-giant, to rot, and without withering away, assume a ghostly patina among the waves. I gazed at it, spellbound by the depravity of the whole thing, and far from eager to pursue the interior.

Early for me, I fell into sleep of a sort, heedless of the ersatz bedding which surrounded my upper body, then swaddled in nothing but rags and fragments I did not bother to arrange about me. I dreamed of Ithaca, of the ripely ebullient forsythia just coming into bloom (May) and the purged blue of the pool. I awoke, but only to recollect how one friend of mine, who had visited me the other year, slept under a patchwork quilt of the periodic table. Lucky he.

It was not a good slumber otherwise, more a surrender of one's being to Hashima and all its cancelled blandishments. I estimate the sleep totaled three hours only, but enough to get me on my feet again for further exploration, to be abandoned as darkness fell.

Back to sleep. The smell, before I nodded off, was of dark woodwork and rancid metal, preparing me for, when I again awoke to brilliant sunshine, a range of six decrepit staircases, each equipped with its own veranda, mounting to another ancillary staircase rising at a forty-five degree angle to nothing at all.

The front of the building had been blown away by some giant's sweep of the all-powerful hand, leaving two samples of rotting stairs and one cobwebbed TV to stare at. Open vertically to the sky, with denuded flanks, only the cascade of steps survived, where once children must have played games, their whole world reduced now to a maze of ramshackle staircases creaking in the wind and ready to fall. One actually did while I gazed.

Torn newspapers and massive chunks of masonry populated the unclimbable steps. The rear of each apartment had collapsed forward, so there was no way up, not that I would have dared. It was as if the masonry had only been kept aloft by prodigious efforts, which had eventually failed. I saw a human skeleton marooned on a high stair, it's face eaten away by obsolete rats I presumed, the legs at inhuman angles to the trunk. Not soon enough, I thought, wondering for a second who and what this non-escapist could be, left behind in the haste to catch the Yokohama boat.

I had never seen such wreckage all around me. Where there stood a surviving balustrade, the whole building had vanished to support it. And I wondered, could this be a natural act of vengeance, a fit of spite before leaving, or was it a product of a century of dereliction, the building left to fall down on its own?

As I extended my early morning tour, I noticed the biggest blocks of masonry still intact, but soon gave my attention instead to a rusty birdcage (no bird), a row of used cups all correctly inverted against the rain. Of course the interiors had been polished in a final act of good faith. Then I saw again: this was a group of perfectly stacked armchairs, every seat broken.

One *sake* bottle, standing forever in a paradise of mold, matched a pair of rubber gloves surmounting a battered briefcase. The gloves were ripped to bits. Best of all, a collection of wrenches, dipped in water, suggested downed tools as one century prepared to yield to the next, while three full bottles of untouched water stood awaiting the first guest on an alcove next to a still-intact window.

THIRTEEN

In our sun there exists a phenomenon popularly called The Random Walk, which sounds inoffensive enough until you realize it refers to how the atoms eventually burst into the open after spending millions of years, some of them, buried deep in the sun, jostling for the way out. This quasi-heroic status of infinitesimal beings may give us pause once we understand it, but it made me wonder why Light Lomax did not do something similar to advertise his whereabouts. No indication of anything, where any slight sign would have worked wonders. *This way, one mile, for instance.* Or *down deep, 140 degrees, five hundred yards.*

But nothing. It was as if he were master-architect Christopher Wren saying, "If you need my whereabouts, look around you." The acme of cheek or self-immersion. With no idea of where to go next, I went nowhere, wondering at his fecklessness. Nothing in my surroundings gave any help, not even the quasi-symbolism of a beer bottle or a mug disguised in the shape of an armchair. Why had I come when I could have been home by now, at ease among the forsythia and the roses?

Then I realized I had not sent word of my imminent arrival. Almost better to predict the doings aboard the sun than to say where *I* was with an entire planet to roam. Therefore, I told myself, make your own way forward as best you can, hoping for a break in the pattern sooner or later. A month later, no doubt. I confronted the massive build-up that surrounded me with its detritus, wondering why Lomax had not returned to the same spot at regular intervals, just to see if I were there. Any body at all. Too much trouble, I decided, and left it at that, heading westward at my own slow pace, hampered by my gear, but resolutely aiming for the zone of maximum visibility, which was not much. I was the proprietor of a mess of rubble, and could easily spend a month searching for Lomax among rank debris, getting tired and tired-er, longing for the boatman's re-arrival to take me off (which I had planned for a week from then, for my food would give out).

West, east, south, and north I tried to find him, but no sign. Perhaps he had abandoned his hopeless quest and returned to the mainland, waiting for the fierce wind to change and guide him back to civilization. I wondered about him incessantly as my supplies dwindled and my walk became slower. You take two eccentrics and set them perambulating, and what do you expect? No good can come of it, not with the one flying a kite and the other prospecting the byways, looking for him. He might have changed his mind and gone to Hong Kong or Sumatra, for all I knew. Even Ithaca to visit his almost forgotten son.

I'd not dreamed of the UFOs for days now, and when I did it was with a certainty that I would never hear their voices in my lifetime.

The world, which I had left behind in a manner of speaking, was such a pitiful mess that I wondered if it ever would come to rights. The number that haunted me was the old 2012, when according to experts the world would end, and 2012 was getting near. I imagined that both he and I would attend the cataclysm in shining modern shoes, black tie new-bought from the panicky tailor down the road, and wait for the intolerable heat to bloat and fry us, neither having found the other on Hashima.

When I finally found Lomax, having made a complete circuit of my surroundings, it was like discovering a human replica. What I found, on closer inspection, after climbing the rafters to make certain (at some risk to life and limb), was nightmarish but obvious. What I thought would be rat-eaten was bee-eaten, in bulk, actually obscuring the lower part of his face. Still his face, but bee-stung.

In fact, he had been eaten alive by some ferocious species, African perhaps, which stings and stings again. The strangest thing was the bees that assailed him still clung to him, dead, but diffusing around him a sweet odor not of honey nor anything like it, more a hint of chloroform. Poor Lomax, to have succumbed thus in the very hour of his archetypal triumph, or whatever restoration he had planned in place of the extinct coal.

When he addressed me, it was in a mumble that I readily associated with some masonry in the act of toppling to its final destination. How could he have spoken when dead? He spoke again, or seemed to, a sound like *goor*, which I assumed, when I recovered from shock, to be the sound of greeting: *good*. Nothing further. I gaped, gasped, and nearly threw up, the combination of his speech with bee-stung lips being too much to bear. I murmured something in return once I regained my composure, and our "conversation" proceeded like this.

"I thought you were dead."

"Only half dead." (I made do with his mumbling, less than sure what he had said, a noise simulating "Ony arf," which was not bad seeing how much he was impeded.)

"You made it after all."

"Yes."

"Only the bees."

"The bastards." (He said in pidgin, "Ba.")

I decided against further conversation and tried to lift him down, careful not to brush against his bee-swollen face. *One. Two. Here we go.* At least, at last, he was free, although not of what ailed him.

After a maze of cell-phoning I hit the right number and secured transport for the next day, provided he survived the night. His face, I now saw, was ballooning and looked close to bursting.

"I heard you," he seemed to say, "fumbling about."

"Fumbling is the right word."

I offered him some cheese and sardines, but he waved all thought of food away, explaining something I could not catch. Clearly, he did not need food, but the therapeutic attentions of a beekeeper on the morrow. How to get him through the night? I propped him up, taking care with his head, and he fell asleep, whether to wake again or not.

Clearly he had been in good spirits. He would not have bothered to climb the rickety face of the building otherwise. So the bees had attacked him while he was active. This made sense, or did it? They might have attacked him on the ground. Apart from his bee-stung face, he seemed all right, but one never knew.

I troughed on the cheese and sardines I had offered him, believing one of us, at least, should keep up our strength, whatever the future held for me. The thought of trekking back with him, via assorted airlines, made me quail, but there was nothing else to do.

As usual, in my improvident way I had no toothpicks for postprandial relief. I longed for strange repasts, buttered soup, for instance, and phosphorescent algae. The weakness of all true gravity disturbed me. Coal harbor was a place of too much work, and not enough stew.

I longed for any placebo to quiet the night stretched out before us like a monster waiting to pounce, and, when I finally drifted off to sleep, it was to dream of being a jet-jockey in a stormy career of incessant ups and downs.

Somehow I got him down the ladder, and made an attempt at equilibrium. For all practical purposes he was blind, maybe forever. His face was a study in the yellow and reds of the countless bees who had attacked him. He groaned with pain at every move. I had almost forgotten what a big man he was, so much so that all my attempts at righting him almost ended in disaster, especially as I concentrated on avoiding where the bees had stung him rather than balancing the true weight on his clumsy feet.

Suffice to say, the leftover goodies, such as they were, remained behind us for the next occupants of the barren coal mine. Sleep for a blind man was no easy matter, since he still felt the pain of being stung, which would go on for days no doubt, perhaps forever. You did not get off lightly with the African bees, which I presumed his assailants were. We spent the night half-sheltered by a decrepit awning, fidgeting (myself), while he tossed and turned as first one puncture, then several, regained striking power, and dreams of ghost bees rose to the fray again, by no means exhausted. I estimated that a hundred bees had done their worst on him and their stingers were still giving him hell. Somehow he managed to control his writhing legs, whereas the pain in his face and eyes remained fairly constant, forcing from him a yelp that multiplied and threatened to become permanent as the night wore on. I survived, of course, and so did he, although I sometimes wondered at his lasting power. How much could he stand before giving out entirely?

The rescue boat arrived early and between us we lugged him down and made him comfortable. Then high speed to the nearest hospital lest he collapse entirely. I theorized that he had been stung only recently and the poison was fresh-minted in his system. What had drawn him up so high in the first place? I had not heard him cry out or otherwise signal.

Now the servant of his physical needs, I wondered where it would reach an end, picturing the return trip to Ithaca, First Class, with him the blind man of the ages. Was he accident prone, a Chernobyl of the bee-stung apocalypse, not to mention his legs?

A wild ride later, and an extravagant tip, we installed him in emergency care and prepared for the worst, which came after three hours when the surgeon, ungloving his hands, explained that the cause was the result of *aggressive mimicry*. The bees were not African, not deadly, although they could sting. And they did. Leave him alone for a week and he would be *as right as rain*, the surgeon said, proud of his English. I paid yet again, and promised myself a visit to the airline office soon.

Why had the phrase "Bamboo Curtain" taken over my mind? Shades of the bridge on the River Kwai. (Not its real name at all, but who cared about geographical etiquette?) I had been there and felt lucky to have survived. Another phrase, "The Weakness of Gravity", haunted my mind in a similar way. Where had it come from? Was gravity weak after all? *What went ye*, I seemed to hear, *out in the wilderness to see?* A man clothed in soft raiment? Indeed yes. I had seen the raiment at my own expense, seen the bees, and now was booked for home at long last.

Airlines come and go, but Lomax stayed on forever, inching his way back to health, well enough anyway to park himself in a lawn chair. I noticed how he seemed to shrink, losing weight in the typical way of the bedridden, as he was for most of the first week, then emerging under his just-shaven beard a mite older, more restrained than usual, and considerably paler. I may be imagining all this, but I doubt it. He had come through all right, but somehow chastened, more serious, more streamlined.

When they let him go at last to Rehab, it was with a disaffected air, that of somebody who had been "through it" and never intended going back for a second dose. The word "coal"

The Invisible Riviera

never passed his lips again, lest he unwittingly trespass into the same black hole. He'd survived snow and blackness, though he looked forward, he said, to next skiing season. I would wait and see. He said this in Japan, and many a thing that's said there goes no further; witness the Japanese habit at Christmas time of recrucifying a six-inch Santa, as anybody could see in the storefront of Nihonbashi, the Japanese equivalent of Harrods.

Here I was killing time and money by waiting for a verdict of perfect health on my old friend, even trying to resolve the UFO problem by thinking of something new to tempt them with. Nothing came of all this ratiocination even when I called it *thinking* instead of the polysyllable. I was through with life. Life fills up with all kinds of extraneous matter, shoving the UFOs aside, spiders on the wing, *eetchy, san,* and *go* (Japanese for 1, 3, 5), all that guff of miscellaneous intercourse which you try hard to forget, but stays implanted in memory until the day you die.

Like *Biddulphia,* a recently acquired word during my wait for Lomax mend. It's a phytoplankton or plant-drifter, otherwise known as *scum,* most evident as a light brown on the walls of fish tanks. I had, initially at any rate, a problem with this word because it reminded me of *Buddha* (see how my mind strayed from the bees to a more wholesome pasture?). I was just getting in the mood for more *Buddha* when the Orientals pronounced Lomax fit to leave the hospital, fit to fly, and all else.

At last, aloft. Lomax disappeared into a magazine entitled *Funeechiwa* (or something such, product of the airline) and I, left to my own devices yet again, made contact with my old friends the UFOs (only in a manner of not speaking of course). Blank followed sleep and blank again. We ate lunch in consummate silence as the plane ground homeward with accustomed zeal. Soon we would be among roses and forsythia, and life would settle again into its old routine of mail by two o'clock, dinner at five, sleep by midnight, but not for Lomax, who had in mind a neglected son and repairs to make.

As for me, I felt some of a reprieve akin to how a walnut feels in the carapace it is sheathed in. Surely the time of the *corrida* was over now, and we could happily go back to ducks and drakes, nearly free of the dark matter that had interrupted our idyll among the countless descendents of Genghis Khan. Better to be vexed by the UFOs again, which have their own peculiar unleavened charm.

There stood the stalwart devotee of Manolo Blahnik in a fresh pair of glittering new shoes, mauve extending to bright purple, which she had saved up for and bought just for our homecoming event. We climbed wearily aboard the car, with little baggage to show, having passed through as many time zones as we could count, and met her smooches with less than primal vigor. But she was feisty and talkative, peppering us with questions which we answered with brief monosyllables, aching to be home at last and postponing the brave *enquêtte* of the morrow to an even later date. How hard was the trip? Average, we replied, doing our best. Do you miss the Kurds? No, it was the Mongols as a matter of fact. How long has the trip taken? Fiercer than ratpower will permit, I answered inconsequentially, while Lomax dozed off in the car on the fringe of morning, relaxing his body all the way and for the first time looking at peace.

Greetings ensued, but paltry, as we headed for bed with "Tell me all about it" ringing in our ears as we mounted the stairs. We left her down below, to wonder why we were so quiet after having traveled so far, First Class and all, giving heed to his scarred face. There must be an unwritten law somewhere on the Rialto that equates the distance you have traveled to the amount you have to say about it, especially the return journey for some reason. We achieved our F for conversation and bedded down where we fell, ready to beat the record for sleeping in. Thus passed into and out of our ken certain memorable moments, forgotten forever in the precipitate onrush of sleep.

The next day passed like a lamb. We again had nothing to say, world travelers par excellence. In spite of urgent questioning by his son and Tabitha, with her husband strangely non-committal, we refused to tell and fobbed people off (including random visitors) with brief rhapsodies about the food and the customs of the natives. We were locked in the presence of an awful, unforgettable dream that thickened up as it became remoter and threatened to engulf us.

We reveled in the cool dry air and the falling catkins and the burly resplendent trees. He and I, sucking up the flora and fauna like two layabouts gathering more and more of the past as the recent future made horrific inroads on our peace of mind, his bees and my bastinado. If it had been unreal, we might not have minded, but it was real, real as blood, and senseless as well. What had been the purpose of our long stay among the Mongols if not to spread the word about them and so extend our view of the world? Was this why we clutched at the greenery of Ithaca with a devotee's frenzy?

Meanwhile, the Japonica shone like coral amid the lesser blooms, yet didn't excite us at all. We had been processed in a larger machine than nature's and needed to recover what brains we had. I mused nonetheless about Lomax and his power of recovery. Perhaps some Aliens were testing him for a proposed project, making him go through the worst only to land him on the other side safe and sound, although remarkably changed within. Perhaps not, and his misfortunes were shared, what all humans in their various guises must go through before biting the dust.

In fact, some were condemned to bite the dust interminably till the end. Lomax was different though, a giant among pygmies, destined for bigger things. I almost said the Aliens were searching for such as him, planning a first landing to honor him and all he stood for, but no, he was too much of a nonbeliever to brook such treatment. Lomax, in his multicolored jump suit, with his massive indoor array of Lego pieces, amassed since he was knee high to a skunk, was a high born dilettante, capable of anything he put his mind to. Which was not always. He could visit Iceland and return without a single comment. Why go there at all? At any rate, he could not claim his sojourn among the Mongols had been dull, or even that it turned out badly in the end. Something was bound to have impressed him, and I looked forward to his eventual summary of the experience, a far cry from my own introverted maunderings. You know what they say: start a man with a diet of UFOs and you have lost him to fiction. If Lomax ever saw the error of his ways and welcomed the silent Aliens, it would be with resounding panache, heavy-handed, no doubt, but decisive and robust.

Already he was past the age of belief in those creatures who so enchanted me and fed me reveries. Perhaps he never would accept them, although a single backyard visit by one of their silent machines would surely be enough to sway him. I left Lomax alone. Hearing Beethoven, where I prefer Delius or Villa-Lobos, I sauntered among what Keats called "the tall-robed senators of mighty woods," envisioning them looking skyward always. The squirrels and rabbits had begun their healing ways, producing absentminded lurches about the yard, as if trying to make up their minds what to do next with so many of nature's sweetmeats to chop at, while overhead the hummingbirds patrolled in lightning dashes the sips they were born for.

"A great writer."
—Hector Bianciotti, front page, *Le Monde*

"One of the most consistently brilliant lyrical writers in America... [West is] possibly our finest living stylist in English."
—*The Chicago Tribune*

"West has been for several decades one of the most consistently brilliant writers in America. His aim seems to be the rendition of an American odyssey analogous to Joyce's union of mythic elements in which earth-mother, shaper-father and offspring, as well as the living and the dead, all achieve communion. The language is Paul West at his best.... shows perfect pitch."
—Frederick Busch, *Chicago Tribune*

"West, prolific novelist and critic, is a literary high-wire artist, performing awe-inspiring aerial feats with language while the rest of us gape up at him in dumb amazement."
—*The Boston Globe*

"Out on those risky ledges where language is continually fought for and renewed—that's where Paul West breathes the thin, necessary air."
—Sven Birkerts, *American Energies*

"A rich, often astonishing meditation upon how a particular human culture can represent a source of 'otherness'—imagination itself—that persists even in a world that other modes of thought and desire have made almost uninhabitable."
—Thomas R. Edwards, *The New York Times Book Review*

"Paul West's epic touches upon the most powerful human themes—the meaning of home, the desecration of war, the quest for a curative past out of spiritual exile."
—Bradford Morrow, *Trinity Fields*

"West's enormous pastiche of yarn-spinning, meditation and sheer wordplay is precisely the sort of work that can help us understand the ways in which we approach and avoid the realities of being human.... Paul West is a worthy custodian of a time-honored tradition."
—Alida Becker, *The Philadelphia Inquirer*

"West's astonishing new novel, which maps the lives of Indians in the American Southwest, reveals a Joycean genius in its exuberant play of language, and its epic and mythic resonances.... West's prose, dazzling in its fecundity, affirms the erotic nature of the literary act."
—*Publisher's Weekly*

"Intoxicated by the novel's unparalleled capacity to connect life and ideas in an unholy mix, he likes fireworks in his fiction, the blow-torch of art that brings reality to the boiling point.... Thorough, passionate, opinionated—West never lets his judgments interfere with his considerable ability to evoke the texture and character of the work under review."
—*Washington Post Book World*

"A writer of distinction and originality."
—*The Los Angeles Times*

"West is an original and daring writer...he has never written anything so risky and triumphant."
—Richard Eder, *Los Angeles Time Book Review*

"No contemporary American prose writer can touch him for sustained rhapsodic invention—he creates a hyperbolic hymn to joy, a swashbuckling swirl of sentences. West stands as an authentic voice in the wilderness, a visionary who plugs the ghosts of history and morality into his textural dream machines."
—*Boston Phoenix*

"In his many works of fiction, memoir, and criticism, West proves himself to be a writer blessed with a cheerfully mordant wit, an acrobatic way with words, ebullient learnedness, and a deep if wry perception of the human

condition. Each previous *Sheer Fiction* volume has offered pleasure, revelation, and provocation, and now, in West's fourth collection of biting literary essays, he again covers a remarkable breadth and complexity of terrain."
—A.L.A. *Booklist*

"West argues passionately for a literature that reveals brilliant minds at work shaping it, that incorporates the world we know today—quantum physics, computer technology.... [His] argument is likely to provoke much disagreement, especially from the academic community... Yet his argument needs to be heard. ...*Sheer Fiction* demands the attention of any reader seriously interested in the purposes of fiction."
—*Wilson Library Bulletin*

"This kind of infectious enthusiasm is rare to the point of non-existence among modern critics. ...Sheer pleasure."
—*Kirkus Reviews*

"The inimitable, brilliant Paul West never ceases to amaze. *Love's Mansion,* orchestrated with Proustian care, offers unforgettable episodes of familial dark and light, bittersweet recollections activated by empathy and sexual awareness. A revelatory book of extraordinary power."
—Walter Abish

"*The Tent of Orange Mist* is a bold, shocking book, filled with cynical brilliance and sensual power."
—*The Boston Review*

"Paul West is one of American literature's most serious and penetrating historical novelists. *The Tent of Orange Mist* is a gorgeous assertion of human life."
—*The San Francisco Chronicle*

"If there are no 'men of letters' any more, there are innumerable figures writing now...who move easily among the fictional, the confessional, the polemical, and the critical. If Paul West is not the most conspicuous of such a group, he is the most stylish and intelligent."
—*Journal of Modern Literature*

"A towering astonishing creation."
—Irving Malin, *Pynchon and Mason & Dixon*

"Paul West's book is transformative. West's immense narrative gift has transformed a traumatic historical event into art. He has re-imagined experience and made literature from it. His book will live."
—Hugh Nissenson, *The Song of the Earth*

"It takes a writer like Paul West to explore the deep psychic lacerations occasioned by [9.11]... Anyone who thinks he or she knows anything about that harrowing moment should read this novel; it will change their perceptions forever."
—David W. Madden, *Understanding Paul West*

""West's phenomenal command of language and the flux of consciousness, and his epic sense of the significance of 9.11 are staggering in their verve, astuteness, and resonance."
—Donna Seaman, *Booklist magazine*

"Not since Proust's *Albertine disparue* has a novel explored the subject of anguish and loss with such unflinching persistency and such annihilating force. This book will have you on tenterhooks and will break your heart."
—Mark Seinfelt, *Final Drafts*

"Paul West, among our more formidable literary intelligences, is not afraid to take risks. His ability to give original expression to complicated ideas about culture and personality is gargantuan. *The Place In Flowers Where Pollen Rests* presents a stunning, hyperbolic vision of men between cultures, between darkness and light, groping for authenticity."
—Dan Cryer, *Newsday*

"Extraordinary in its scope, inventiveness, and prose.... spectacular writing."
—Gail Pool, *Cleveland Plain Dealer*

"An exciting and evocative tale of love and treason."
—Andrew Ervin, *The Philadelphia Inquirer*

"While this biting, scatological tour de force will appeal mostly to West fans and more experimental poetry readers (many of whom are already West fans), it deserves a prominent place in poetry collections."
—Rochelle Ratner, *Library Journal*

"An exhilarating collection.... West's genuine excitement for this fiction is contagious and his own language is as splendid."
—*Review of Contemporary Fiction*

"[This novel] thrusts us into a rich domestic situation that reflects the complexities of our century like a prism. *Love's Mansion* is the late 20th century's contribution to the great, classical love novels of history."
—Elena Castedo

"[*The Tent of Orange Mist*] is both a terror and a joy to read."
—Kathryn Harrison

"The rest of us will despair of ever being able to write prose so immaculate as that of Paul West."
—Jonathan Yardley

"Most intriguing is the overarching narration told by Osiris, god of the Nile, who comments on this swarm of events with hilarious and humane authority. Profound and entertaining, *Cheops: A Cupboard for the Sun* is perhaps Paul West's greatest novel yet."
—J. M. Adams

"West, a writer of finesse, amplitude, and wit…describes his father in startlingly tactile detail as he recounts the wrenching war stories his father told him…. West's sensitivity to the vagaries of temperament is exquisite, his tenderness deeply moving. Writing of wars past in a time of war, West creates a portrait of his father that has all the richness of Rembrandt as it evokes the endless suffering wars precipitate."
—Donna Seaman, *Booklist*

"For beautiful sentences fed on brainpower, there is perhaps no other contemporary writer who can match him."
—Albert Mobilio, *Salon.com, Reader's Guide to Contemporary Authors*